Waiting
for Stalin
to Die

Essential Prose Series 133

Canada Council
for the Arts

Conseil des Arts
du Canada

ONTARIO ARTS COUNCIL
CONSEIL DES ARTS DE L'ONTARIO

an Ontario government agency
un organisme du gouvernement de l'Ontario

Guernica Editions Inc. acknowledges the support of the Canada Council
for the Arts and the Ontario Arts Council. The Ontario Arts Council
is an agency of the Government of Ontario.

We acknowledge the financial support of the Government of Canada.

Waiting for Stalin to Die

Irene Guilford

**GUERNICA
EDITIONS**
TORONTO · BUFFALO · LANCASTER (U.K.)
2017

Michael Mirolla, editor
David Moratto, interior and cover design
Guernica Editions Inc.
1569 Heritage Way, Oakville, (ON), Canada L6M 2Z7
2250 Military Road, Tonawanda, N.Y. 14150-6000 U.S.A.
www.guernicaeditions.com

Distributors:
University of Toronto Press Distribution,
5201 Dufferin Street, Toronto (ON), Canada M3H 5T8
Gazelle Book Services, White Cross Mills,
High Town, Lancaster LA1 4XS U.K.

First edition.
Printed in Canada.

Legal Deposit—First Quarter
Library of Congress Catalog Card Number: 2016959322
Library and Archives Canada Cataloguing in Publication
Guilford, Irene, author
Waiting for Stalin to die / Irene Guilford. -- First edition.

(Essential prose series ; 133)
Issued in print and electronic formats.
ISBN 978-1-77183-153-6 (paperback).--ISBN 978-1-77183-154-3 (epub).
--ISBN 978-1-77183-155-0 (mobi).

I. Title. II. Series: Essential prose series ; 133

PS8563.U543W35 2017   C813'.54   C2016-907227-4   C2016-907228-2 *for Nigel*

VYTAS

TORONTO

1949

*He dreams of Vilnius. Night after night he dreams
of the city which he left, though he did not wish to.
And he dreams of Lidia, his lost love.*

*Waking in the dark, he sits up in bed, arms around
his knees. He gnaws the backs of his hands. He chews
the inside of his lips and cheeks. He eats his grief,
taking it into himself like food.*

*Lidia. If we had not left she would not be lost.
In the morning, the dream is gone. His home.
His love. His life.*

Chapter 1

T hough not a joking man, Vytas would say years later that he had become a doctor again by accident. Surrounded by family in his Baby Point garden, sitting in the deep greenery, he would tell a story which happened to be true. His three married daughters would be setting out a summer lunch. His three sons-in-law would lift their heads from quiet political talk. And while the grandchildren sat at his feet, spellbound by events, the adults heard the oceans of meaning behind the words.

Every Sunday morning, I used to walk in High Park.

He had stopped before Lidia's picture as always before going out. Gazing at her love-filled face, aching for her presence in just the next room, he turned his Swiss army knife over and over in his pocket. Won't be long, he wanted to call out. And hefting the smooth red enamel handle, feeling the weight of the blades hidden inside, he wondered if he would become one of those lonely old bachelors who absentmindedly jingled coins in their trouser pockets.

He had stood at Hilltop Gardens, looking out over Grenadier Pond. The British Grenadiers had gone through the ice on their way to fight the Americans in 1812. This history was not his. His lived in a faraway land. He carried it inside him. And looking down at the large red Maple Leaf Garden, he felt surrounded by a history without meaning.

He descended to a pond at the park's heart, a dark shallow pool where people threw bread to the ducks. Walking along the rim, head bent, tread rhythmic, he would think of Lidia. The smooth green water calmed and soothed. In these moments, memory sweetened rather than stung. And pausing, looking up, he would squint past the sunlight piercing through the leaves.

A father and young daughter entered along Spring Road, a short stump of a street off Parkside Drive. Wearing a white shirt, fine grey slacks and expensive loafers, the man moved with ease. Even from a distance, Vytas could tell they were moneyed people. He sensed the man's casual belonging. And conscious of his brown and white pinstriped suit from the DP camps, Vytas felt himself to be the outsider that he was.

The little girl skipped alongside her father in a yellow sundress and black patent leather shoes. Approaching the pond, she tossed bread onto the dark surface of the water. Ducks snatched at the bobbing bits. The child clapped her hands in delight. And in the joyful look she turned towards her father, Vytas saw an untroubled childhood, a home secure and safe.

The father tipped a brown paper bag towards his daughter, offering her a plum. Sitting side by side on the low stone wall, they ate fruit. Juice dribbled down the girl's chin. The father wiped it away. And holding out his palm, he waited for the plum stone.

Spit, Vytas could see the father mouth.

Plums. How Vytas had loved them as a boy.

His uncle's strong hands had lifted him up into the orchard trees, holding him by the waist as he reached past scratchy branches to twist free a plump fruit. Trailing behind his mother and her brother, biting through the purple skin to the golden flesh beneath, he had heard drifting snatches of conversation. You must come with us, she had said. And watching his uncle shaking his head, slow and sad, he knew it would be their last visit.

The little girl shrieked with excitement and pointed. A swan was swimming in their direction. She dashed towards it. Stop, the father cried, pounding after the child with a plum stone still in her mouth. Stop!

She pulled up short. She fell to the pavement with a soft thud.

Vytas raced towards her. He dropped to one knee. She was rasping for air. Her face was becoming purple. Her eyes were rolling back in their sockets. He had, at most, one minute.

"Doctor," he said, jabbing at his chest.

Frozen, the white-faced father nodded.

Vytas opened his Swiss army knife. He cut a small slit in the girl's throat. He tossed aside the ink cartridge from his ballpoint pen. He slid the hollow tube into her trachea. The girl sucked air. Her chest heaved. And watching the purple fading from her face, he sat back on his heels in relief.

"Ambulance," Vytas said to the stunned father, who took off towards Parkside Drive.

Vytas crouched beside the child, holding both her hands in one of his. He stroked her hair. He smiled into her frightened eyes. And keeping her still, he murmured to her in Lithuanian.

Nebijok, pupele. Don't be afraid, little one.

It was late afternoon when Vytas returned home. Only after climbing into the ambulance with Mr. Taylor and Anita to accompany them to the hospital, only after assuring the grateful father that his child could be safely released, only then had he, too, been allowed to go home. He climbed the stairs to his room. He shut the door. And lifting Lidia's photo to his lips, he kissed it.

Mr. Taylor happened to be the Taylor of Gordon and Taylor, Barristers and Solicitors. He lived on High Park Gardens, next door to Dr. Griffin, dean of the Medical School. On Sunday morning, the two men stood talking on their sunlit lawns. As Mr. Taylor described the swift actions of the young foreigner who had saved his daughter's life, Dr. Griffin's eyes widened. Always on the lookout for quick-thinking young doctors, the dean said, Send him to me.

Later that day, while Vytas and his parents were eating lunch in their landlady's kitchen, the phone rang. Lifting their heads from their food, they wondered who would interrupt a Sunday family meal. Their landlady answered. She said it was for Vytas. And wiping his mouth with a paper napkin, he rose to see who was calling.

It was Mr. Taylor. He wanted Vytas to meet Dr. Griffin. In gratitude for services rendered, one good turn deserving another, so to speak.

Vytas gripped the receiver. As the words rolled over him, he grasped at phrases he didn't understand. Nevertheless he got the gist. *Medical School. Chance.* And holding the receiver to his ear, he felt the pulsing future.

⌒⊙⌒

His mother Juze was a sparkling creature, small, compact and fiery, warm-hearted and kind. She was also shrewd, her wits having saved son and husband from danger more than once. A coy smile at an officer. A bit of charm in the right place. Her lover, Alex, had had been killed in the war. Vytas was the unborn child he had never seen. Grief had transmuted into a passion, rivalling no other, for the child of a lover who lay dead in a field.

It was Brunius, not Alex, who had descended from the train. Coming towards her on the crowded station platform in Vilnius, taking her hand, he had given her the news. She had slumped against him. And there she had remained. After a short, respectful courtship, they had married, united by a battlefield promise made to a dying comrade.

Brunius, twenty years her senior, was an old soldier, tall, spare and reserved. Seeing her holding her new-born son, her face blazing with love, he knew he would never come first for mother or child. What life gives, he thought, it can just as easily take away. And knowing himself to be honoured and respected, he was abashed at the treasures life had swept up on his shores.

They lived in harmony, the child a goodness arising from crushed lives. Advancing their son's happiness became their chief joy. Vytas entered medical school. He became engaged to Lidia, daughter of old friends. And anticipating graduation, a wedding and grandchildren, their hearts were full.

Then war came. Sitting around a Sunday luncheon table, hearing the guns of the advancing Russian front, they spoke in hushed tones. We must leave, they said. Whatever happens will happen to all of us. And looking into one another's eyes, they saw feelings impossible to express.

The two families had reached Berlin. Fighting through crowds on the station platform, clambering aboard a west-bound train, they had secured seats. The train would take them further from danger. It would leave in four hours. And rejoicing at having come this far without misfortune, they settled in to wait.

It was then that Lidia's mother had lifted her hand to her throat with a small cry. The little cross which she had received as a little girl from a mother now dead, a gold cross which could be bartered for food, was gone. It must have come off while they slept. It must be among the pillows. They must go back and look.

Hurry, Juze had said to Lidia's parents. We will wait for you. We will save your seats.

I'll be back soon, Lidia had whispered against Vytas' ear.

Vytas had watched through every minute of every hour, his teeth clenched, his eyes straining for his love's return. When the train had lurched into motion, he had leapt up. Lidia! Lidia! he had cried. And trying to climb out the window, clambering after his escaping words, he felt his mother grip the back of his shirt.

No! she had cried, pulling him back with a ferocity he had never known. No. You mustn't. They will catch up with us. They will find us. Come away from the window, my son. Come away.

He had let himself be turned back into the gloom of the compartment. Resting his forehead against the cold window, staring into the black night, he had heard the rhythmic clacking of the wheels. Lidia Lidia Lidia, they had said. And carried through a darkened countryside he could no longer see, he travelled towards safety and away from love.

Much later in Canada, they would learn that Lidia and her parents had walked into the arms of the enemy which had just entered Berlin. They would have been shipped back the way they had come. They would have been sent to Siberia, put in prison or been shot. They were never seen or heard from again.

The guilt never left Vytas. He lived in a dark tunnel leading back to Siberia, prison or death. He should not have let her go. He should have gone with her. He should have gone after her when she did not return. He should be with her, there, in the dark heart of the earth. Light and life lay before him, but forgiveness was out of reach.

Vytas descended from the College streetcar, stepping into the fine city morning. Standing on the sidewalk in the clear spring air, he looked across the street. A pale dirt path led to the university. It cut between old buildings of rough grey stone. And imagining his arrival in front of the medical building, his heart stirred at the prospect of a life resumed.

Men moved past him with ease in early morning. Walking with purpose, intent on business, they acknowledged ladies with the quick lift of a hat. They would stop to shake a man's hand. They would grip his upper arm. And continuing on their way, they passed unawares through the invisible tethers around Vytas, soft translucent ribbons tying him to a country they didn't know.

His mother was waiting in the flat on Glenlake Avenue.

Standing by the second-floor window, looking down into the street, she would watch for him to round the corner. He would turn away from the commotion of Dundas Street and the railway tracks. He would enter the peaceful eddy of the quiet, treed street. And watching him come into view, she waited for him to reach home.

Home? Lithuania was home. Canada was safety and freedom, struggle and hope, disappointment and hard work and the occasional helping hand which, just because it was needed, stung the pride. It was no longer running and hiding as it had been during the war, or limbo as it had been in the DP camps. It was not death or imprisonment or Siberia, as it was for those who had not left soon enough, or run far enough, or stayed behind. It was life by grit and good luck, a life for which they were grateful.

The streetcar clanged at a young woman crossing in front. Jumping at the loud sudden peal, she hurried past in her swirling skirt and white high-heeled shoes. She cast a good-natured smile at the driver. She gave him a friendly wave. And in her light-hearted movements and manner, Vytas saw his Lidia.

He hesitated to cross the street. It felt like betrayal to step from darkness into light.

Gentle hands nudged his back, the soft unseen hands of ghosts. In the pearly morning light, a voice whispered. Go, she said. Go. And feeling a soft push, he stepped off the curb.

Chapter 2

O na stood in the doorway of the second-floor bedroom, watching Juze sorting clothes on the bed. Hoping for a chat with the doctor's mother, she hovered. In Lithuania they would never have met. In Canada, Juze was a tenant in her house. And watching her lifting and examining Vytas' shirt, Ona thought what a good catch the son would be for her daughter.

"Juze, what's your boy's favourite dish?"

"You're such a fine cook, *Šeimininke*. It's a pleasure to eat your food. Please don't put yourself out for Vytas. He's too busy studying to notice what he eats."

Šeimininkė. Landlady.

If Ona had encountered Juze in the village, she would have stepped down into the street. Farmer's wife, she would have allowed the doctor's mother to pass. She would have waited, head lowered. She might have received an acknowledging nod. And standing in the bedroom doorway of her house in a new country, watching the woman's disregard as she folded her son's clothes, Ona knew that the old ways still held.

The house was on Glenlake, five doors away from Dundas and the CN/CP railway lines running alongside. Rounding the corner, she could walk to the IGA for butter and eggs, to the Towers beyond Bloor for plastic flowers, to the Village Deli at the top of Roncesvalles for unsmoked ham. She could stop at Margis Pharmacy for a chat. Mr. Margis was Lithuanian. And crossing the threshold of his shop, passing through a doorway set on an angle, she could step into the fields of home.

Ona and Jonas had bought the house within one year of arrival, receiving help from a *senas imigrantas*, an immigrant from the 1930's. Providing the down payment of five hundred dollars, the rotund middle-aged bachelor might have harboured hopes of marrying the fresh young daughter. Danguole would not have it. The suitor had slipped away. And paying the loan from Jonas' factory wages, faithfully month by month, they honoured an arrangement made, and kept, on trust.

"I want someone handsome and young," Danguole had said. "Not some old man."

"Stupid as well as spoiled," Ona had said.

Danguole. What a fancy name for a child. Who needed a name like that on a farm? After the name came leather shoes costing two sacks of grain, a leather satchel for school and a bicycle which the girl had paraded before her friends, nose in the air. You're spoiling her rotten, Ona had said to Jonas. Waving her away, he had returned to farming and the solace of drink.

Her father had married her to Jonas, the second son of the farmer across the road. Returning from his neighbour's, flinging his sheepskin coat aside, he had announced the arrangements. He would get a son-in-law to help with the land. Jonas would get a farm of his own. And Ona, part of the settlement along with the chickens, horses and pigs, would get a husband.

In Canada, they had nothing. Who would want Danguole, this spoiled child, simply for herself?

With a shrug, she left the doctor's mother folding her precious son's trousers. Going back downstairs, she entered the kitchen in which they mainly lived. A curtain split the two remaining rooms into living room and bedroom. Two single beds, the headboards pushed against the fabric, were for her and Jonas. Danguole slept on a small couch by the wall. A chamber pot served them at night and in the morning, leaving the single second-floor bathroom free for the tenants.

"Always let the doctor go first," Ona told Danguole.

Anything could happen with two young people brushing up against one another on the stairs every day. The doctor might not be interested in her daughter yet—well who would be, a silly girl like that—but Danguole was not bad-looking, plump once again after years of little food. She could be pleasing enough if she wanted. The doctor would be quite a catch for the family. And in old age, it would be handy having him in the house.

"Hurry up. What kind of wife will you make for the doctor," she said, watching her daughter getting down on her hands and knees to pull the chamber pot out from under the bed.

"But he doesn't like me," Danguole said, her thumb firmly fixed on the stained cardboard cover cut to fit.

Her highly developed radar, skilled at homing in on anyone well-disposed towards her, knew that the doctor was not interested. His words and smiles were only politeness. When his look landed upon her, it slid away. Even she knew that a farm girl could not snare a doctor.

"Do you think my husband liked me?" Ona said, waving a wooden spoon.

Jonas had raged around the house, drunk. Circling the outside, he'd smashed windows. He'd chased her into the fields until she fell. He'd stood over her, a rock held high over his head. If, in the end, he'd merely beaten her black and blue, such was life.

"But what about Lidia?" Danguole had seen the doctor's sad distant look.

"Lidia's not here. You are. What man won't take warm flesh over a cold ghost?"

At that moment, taking a break from his studies, Vytas came into the kitchen. Seeing mother and daughter together, working amid the peaceful burble of steaming pots, his face softened. Ona had seen that look on farm labourers come to the door for a drink of water at midday. She understood the unchanging attraction of family and food. And imagining him already as her son-in-law, she turned upon him an earthly, ribald charm.

"Come in, Doctor. Come join us women."

"I'm not a doctor yet."

He had tried more than once to dissuade her from using a title not yet his, but to no avail. What could you say to a woman like that? Nothing. You just let her talk. He smiled down at his shoes.

"Oh, you will always be Doctor to me. Danguole, where are your manners? Make the doctor some tea."

Ona watched her daughter hurrying to wipe her hands on her apron. Seeing her put the kettle on the stove then make to join the doctor at the table, Ona stopped her with a look. Don't you know anything? Wait on him. Serve him. Don't sit next to him. Not yet. And lowering herself into a chair beside the doctor, she started talking about who was marrying whom.

"Everyone seems to be marrying these days," Ona said.

"Mother, please," Danguole whispered, her eyes lowered.

"What of it daughter?" Ona said. "Everyone marries sooner or later."

Vytas glanced into the pleasantly sunlit back garden. He could ask the girl to sit on the steps. Just for a few moments. Just to get her away from her mother. Feeling her longing look, he thought better of it.

Danguole bent towards him, pouring tea. Her body emanated heat. A dark drop hung from the spout. She caught it with one finger. Putting it to her mouth, she gave him a secret smile.

Just a matter of time, Ona thought.

Juze had heard Vytas go downstairs. Following him to the kitchen, she saw her son seated between a mother engaging him in conversation and a daughter leaning in to refill his cup. So that's what the old hag's up to, she thought. Well, if she's hoping for a marriage between our children, she can hope forever. Even for a farm woman, that's very foolish.

"Shouldn't you be working, Vyteli?"

"Just finishing my tea, Mother."

Rising, he drained his teacup in elaborate silence, then left.

All was not perfection then between mother and son, Ona thought. Opportunity leapt into view.

"You work your boy hard."

"No harder than you work your daughter, *Šeimininke*."

Šeimininkė. Housekeeper. There it was again. Well, Miss High and Mighty Mother-of-a-precious doctor, we'll see what life brings.

"Isn't it time he had a wife to help him?"

"He is well taken care of."

"I mean someone other than a mother. Now take my daughter Danguole. She's a little foolish but not a bad girl. A hard worker. Not bad looking either. What more could a man want?"

She sent Juze a roguish look. We women know what we are about. We know how it's done.

Juze pulled back, appalled. This may be how you do things on the farm, but my son for your daughter? Never. He's meant for better things than marriage to a foolish farm girl.

Oh no? Ona thought. Just you wait and see.

Danguole stood at the sink in the ill-lit corner. Washing up, rattling the cups, she tried not to hear the conversation. She would have climbed into the darkness if she could. She wanted to get away from her mother. All I want is a family, she thought. With husband, children and home, she would be happy and loved.

⁓

Ona prepared a surprise lunch for her tenants, especially for Vytas, future doctor and prospective son-in-law. Rejecting *zrazai*, beef rolls filled with minced veal, pork and mushrooms, she had settled on *cepelinai,* potato dumplings served with crispy fried bacon bits and cool sour cream. There was nothing wrong with simple food. It would show their frugality. When the doctor became her son-in-law, there would be time enough for steak.

Danguole worked in the kitchen, preparing the dumplings. Waiting for a large pot of water to boil, she grated potatoes. Her face was moist and flushed. Her fine hair hung limp. Ona looked with distaste at her daughter's appearance.

"He's not going to want you for yourself so you'd better show what you can do in the kitchen. When he arrives, greet him first. Seat him in the centre. Offer food. Don't make him ask. Serve him before everyone else. Make sure his plate is never empty. Treat him like a king. And don't sit down at the table yourself. You can eat afterwards. Now go clean yourself up."

Ona went looking for Jonas. He was sitting in the living room, reading the newspaper and smoking his Craven 'A' cigarettes. He wore a clean green plaid shirt. His wet hair was neatly parted and combed. She stood the doorway, brandishing her wooden spoon.

"Cut the grass," she said.

"You stick to your business, woman, and I'll stick to mine."

He stubbed out his cigarette and rose. With a grunt, she returned to the kitchen.

Vytas and his parents came back from mass to find the lawn cut, the table set and the landlords waiting in the kitchen, the daughter in a white blouse, face freshly washed, hair smoothed back.

"Please sit down, Doctor," Ona said.

He let himself be led to the place of honour. Jonas and Ona slipped into seats on either side of him. His parents were left to take up what spots remained. Danguole was left standing.

"Pour the drinks, Jonai," Ona said.

Jonas needed no encouragement. He poured rye into small shot glasses.

"To the young doctor," he said, raising his glass.

"To young people," Ona said, lifting hers with a knowing look.

Danguole reddened. Vytas turned away, slightly embarrassed.

Juze watched Danguole hurrying between table and stove. Ladling out dumplings, spooning bacon bits over top, she grew hot and flustered. Such a silly girl, Juze thought. Sillier still to think of marrying my Vytas. Seeing her son taking no notice of Danguole's efforts to please, she turned to her food which, she had to admit, was very good. As a cook, Ona deserved her reputation.

"Thank you for lunch, *Šeimininke*," she said the moment they were finished.

"You can't go yet!" Ona said. "There's cake."

Oh, yes, we can, Juze thought. Feeling her husband's touch on her arm, she glanced down at his face. Be patient, his look said. Be kind. With a small sigh, she sat back down.

Ona served *medaunykas*, a dark dense honey cake. Cutting through the glistening surface, she passed round thick slices. The doctor used his fingers. Just a matter of time, she thought, watching him licking at the sticky residue that no napkin could remove. And sitting back, she allowed herself a satisfied smile.

If she thinks my son is going to be caught like some fly, Juze thought, she's crazy. *Kvaila.* Jonas wasn't bad but the wife and daughter were impossible.

"Well really the time has come to go," Juze said, rising with determination once the cake was eaten. "Vytas must study."

"Mother," Vytas said, "there is still coffee."

Danguole shot him a look of gratitude. She served the coffee without spilling, though her hands trembled so.

Finally the luncheon was over. The parties rose from the table with contented sighs, declaring it a fine meal. Brunius praised the *cepelinai*, saying he had never eaten better. Juze echoed simple, empty words. Nice. Very nice. She couldn't wait to get away from this unwanted hospitality.

"Thank you for your hospitality," Vytas said, taking Ona's hand.

"*Nėra už ką,*" she said, flushing at his sincerity. It was nothing.

Vytas turned to Danguole, also taking her hand in his. Her face flushing also, she lowered her eyes. He put his other hand on top of hers. For a moment, he let it rest. A sudden silence descended upon the two sets of parents watching the young couple.

"Come anytime," Jonas said, clapping Brunius on the back. "Come when the women are away. We'll have a drink together. Just us men."

Brunius laughed in soldierly camaraderie. Juze waited stone-faced. Vytas smiled in friendliness at nothing and everything.

Just a matter of time, Ona thought. Just a matter of time.

Ona lay in bed that night, considering her daughter's prospects. Speaking across a divide larger than the space between their two beds, she addressed her husband. The doctor had held her daughter's hand in both of his. He had smiled into her eyes. Marriage was a distinct possibility.

"What do you think?" she said.

"Don't be stupid, woman."

"Stupid? Anything's possible between two young people."

Silence filled the space between the two beds.

"It's a foolish idea," he eventually said.

Foolish? She had been called foolish when, on the run in Germany, she had set off on foot across the fields, carrying their bucket of lard. Approaching a farm, she had found only the wife. She had bartered. What did men know? she had thought, returning with bread and eggs to husband, daughter and wagon.

"Do something. Talk to the father," she said, remembering her father's trip to the farmer across the road.

"I can't make the man fall in love with our daughter," he said.

"Love," Ona snorted. "What would you know about love?"

Jonas heaved himself over and fell asleep.

Danguole lay on her couch, listening to the discussion of her future. Hearing her father's heavy breathing as he settled into sleep, listening to the clack of her mother's rosary beads, Danguole felt a vague stirring of hope. Perhaps her mother was right. Perhaps a doctor could be hers after all. Please God, she prayed, bring me love. And murmuring her own private prayers, she too fell asleep.

Chapter 3

Vytas sat in his room, studying at a table overlooking the back garden. Amid books lying open atop one another, thick books on anatomy and physiology, he studied as he had never studied before. He studied with the ferocity of second chances. He studied on behalf of lives lost. And squinting as if trying to discern a face through a mesh screen, he studied old material through a new language.

He was aware of his double-breasted suit hanging on a hook on the door, his polished shoes waiting side by side under the bed. Putting them on every morning before going to the university, these kindnesses from the DP camp in Germany and the Women's committee in Toronto, he was grateful. They covered the reality pulsing inside. And sitting on his bed, bending to tie his shoes, he was glad of the false exterior which allowed him to function in the outside world.

Going on rounds at the hospital, white-coated among other student doctors, he would think of his colleagues back in Vilnius. Sitting afterwards in his landlady's kitchen or in the living room with his landlord, he would think of private gatherings with family and friends. He had new acquaintances. He had the comfort of compatriots. And looking around at those who had lost more than just love, he was grateful for his parents.

Vyteli, don't you think you should be studying?

His mother's words had irked him. It was not what she'd said but that she'd said it in front of Ona and Danguole. He was not a small boy who needed constant watching. He was a grown man. He didn't need to be told what to do.

He lifted his head from his studies, looking out at the garden. Jonas kept the lawn mown to green velvet perfection. In the narrow beds running down either side, Ona grew roses, peonies and dahlias, tomatoes, green onions and dill. The couple worked together, bending to their labours. They touched the comfort of the earth. And standing under the arc of trees at the bottom of the garden, Ona in her striped housedress, Jonas in his singlet, they would talk in the quiet peacefulness of evening.

Once, Ona had taken Vytas by the hand, leading him to a tomato plant. Bending in the bright sunshine, she had lifted a leaf. She had revealed the fruit beneath. It was red and ripe. And turning toward him, her face had been wide with wonder at the mysteries of life.

Danguole came out into the garden, carrying a bowl and knife. Bending to cut green onions, her hair falling into her face, her blouse coming out of her skirt, she looked hot, harassed and unhappy. Poor girl, he thought. It was hard not to feel sorry for her. Perhaps she would find someone to love, someone to love her. Everyone needed love, people like her perhaps more than most.

She straightened. Lifting one hand to shield her eyes against the sharp sun, she peered up at his window. He drew back into the shadows. Better to keep a distance, he thought.

Better not to encourage. And settling back at his table, he resumed his studies.

⁓

One particularly intense day in Vilnius Hospital, he had wanted relief from the clinical whiteness, the grey linoleum, the long hallways echoing with footsteps running in crisis. Wishing a few moments respite from sickness and death, he went to the art gallery. He wanted to see the red lips of courtesans, the plump limbs of cherubs, the coy turn of an angel's head. He'd wanted life and beauty, to sense the impetus behind the brush. And there, he had caught sight of her.

Lidia.

She came in with a crowd of fellow students, carried upon conviviality. Shining with sociability, she had caught sight of him. She had turned towards a young man in a blazer and striped wool scarf. Who *is* that? Vytas would learn that she had asked the fellow student. And listening head bent, she kept casting Vytas shy glances.

His eyes followed her graceful movement among friends. Turning to smile at him, her dark chignon shifting atop her head, she was relaxed and easy. How I wish I could be like that, he thought. How I wish I could meet someone like that. And at that moment she fixed him with a look, a beam of light upon which he could walk.

Almost without knowing it, he began travelling towards her. Reaching her in resumed conversation with friends, he paused at her back. She quivered and turned towards him. I am Lidia, she said, her voice shimmering like summer heat. And he knew he had reached a place he would never leave.

She was studying at the Vilnius Academy of Fine Arts. Watched over by loving parents, encircled by lively interest, she had become the woman who now took his hand. Warmth filled his body. He closed his eyes in rapture. They left together, her with a sparkling wave to her friends, him in the happy daze of being captured.

She would go to the river to paint, striding to the water's edge. Following her through the tall grasses, he would carry her easel and paints. Hands on hips, she would take in the air. Then she would work. And settling himself down on the ground, watching her effortless movement between life and art, he felt the blissful trust of being forgotten.

Every Sunday morning Vytas and his parents went to church. Waiting at the streetcar stop, his mother in a flared, three-quarter length cream-coloured coat, his father in the brown tweed jacket and tan sweater vest, they would watch the Dundas car approach. It would whoosh to a heavy halt. The doors would clatter open. And grasping the slippery metal pole and pulling themselves up, they would settle on the red leather seats.

The streetcar would cross Bloor, curving left at the top of Roncesvalles. Rising at the bridge at Sorauren, it would lift them over factories, lands and railway lines lying beneath. They would pass Lansdowne, Dufferin, Dovercourt, and Ossington, looking down streets at homes that held lives they could not imagine. They would reach Trinity Bellwoods Park, the long stretch of green a relief after the concrete. And arriving at Gore Vale Avenue and the church, they would alight amongst their people.

The church was crowded, often standing room only. Coming for comfort, community and warmth, exiles prayed that one day their country would be free. Their hope was fervent. Their belief was cast iron. And organizing, building and remembering, they kept their homeland alive in their hearts.

Vytas knelt, praying for Lidia. As Father Geras passed from confession booth to altar, his robes swishing, Vytas prayed for Lidia to be alive. As the priest raised his arms in benediction, wide white sleeves sliding back, Vytas prayed that she was with people she loved. When he genuflected to the sharp ringing of altar bells, Vytas prayed that she be kept safe. He prayed to see her again. If God was capable of miracles, Vytas was capable of faith.

After mass, the congregation spilled onto the church steps for news and gossip. They rejoiced over a recent letter from Lithuania, crowing at censors too stupid to catch the clever allusions written into the lines. Amid triumph and tears, they showed around a miraculously-arrived brother. With collective gravity, they sighed that times were bad. Then uplifted by sunshine, prayers and hope, they set off for Lithuania House and lunch.

They ambled along Dundas in amiable companionship. Talking of jobs, homes and politics, they walked the three stoplights to Ossington. They would never spend money on streetcar tickets for such a short distance. They had crossed Europe on foot and still had two good legs. And saying their friendly farewells at the door, they would go upstairs to the second floor for a Sunday meal or return home for lunches of their own.

One Sunday, Vytas saw an old man making his way through the crowd on the church steps. Approaching one person after another, placing his hand on an arm, his manner was humble and deferential. He was looking for someone. A woman turned and pointed out Vytas. And feeling the man's gaze land upon him, Vytas' thoughts raced towards the relief of knowledge while scrabbling away from its terror.

The man stopped before him. He was not old, just encrusted with suffering, a pebbly surface that could not be scrubbed off. His eyes held the vastness of the ocean he had just crossed. And drawing Vytas aside, taking him into the park and the private shade of trees, he delivered his news.

⌘

He had come upon them in winter. Shipped eastwards by truck then northwards by rail, they had been set down on foot in the snow. Men rode alongside, high on horseback, their greatcoats spread over the horses' rumps. They drove the marchers on. They left the fallen face-down in the snow. It was a death march into Siberian winter.

Lidia and her parents trudged forward, their faces wrapped in rags that had once been their clothing, the tatters flapping wildly in the wind. Their fingers and lips were black from frostbite. Each night they huddled together to sleep, certain they would die. Each morning they woke, their hair stuck to ice. They starved but they did not yet die.

He had tried to convince them to escape with him, their chances no worse than the certainty of a death march. The parents urged their daughter to go. She had shaken her head with a sad smile. No, she would not forsake her parents. Drawing even closer, they became one body edging towards death.

The night of his departure, she gave him a message.

If you find Vytas, tell him that I love him. Tell him that he is always with me. Tell him not to mourn me for too long. Tell him not to forget me. Tell him to love again.

For four years, the old man carried the carefully-guarded words, repeated faithfully night after night before sleep. Discharging his holy mission, he set them down before Vytas like stones. Vytas stooped to pick them up. They pulsed with life in in his palms. And as the last of her love passed into him, a great roar pushed the world aside.

He looked up into the oak tree, his heart aching so that he thought he would die. Squinting against the sharp light jabbing through the leaves, he followed the branches skyward. He wanted to climb into those strong limbs. He wanted to live in their embrace. And closing his eyes, he longed to disappear into forest sunshine forever.

⌒✿⌒

Vytas fell into a pit so dark and deep that Juze began to fear he might not recover. Not in their days of running, not even at the train station when they had pulled him away from the window had he been so despondent. There had been only survival. There had been hope. Now he slept in snatches, ate little and worked not all.

"Work, Vyteli, you must work," she urged. "If not for yourself, then for her. Especially for her. So that it will not have been in vain."

He resumed his work, his heart hanging like a lead anchor inside his chest. Studying at his desk, hearing the slam of cupboard doors or the rush of running water from the kitchen below, he knew she was right. They were alive. They were safe. They were free. And life was continuing.

When memory ambushed him at night, he did not fight it. Pressing his face into his pillow, he would turn to the soft darkness where he could still feel her. He had lost her in life. He would not lose her in death. Welcoming grief, he held her close.

The household kept a quiet and respectful distance. Ona made his favourite food—*kugelis*, potato pudding. Jonas offered the newspaper before reading it himself. Danguole left him alone. She followed his movements with watchful eyes. When he started his solitary walks in High Park, they sighed with collective relief.

He walked, placing one foot in front of the other. Staring down at his shoes, seeing their tips coming in and out of view, they seemed not to be his. He walked through the greenness of July, the gold of August, the freshness of September and a rustling, leafy October. He passed through a grey November and entered the swirling whiteness of winter. He followed her steps in the snow, placing his feet in her hollows. Then the footprints ended. And there he placed his heart.

He passed his exams, becoming a doctor once again. Establishing an office on the main floor of a building on Bloor Street, he had a waiting room crowded with patients eager to consult this young doctor of whom they were so proud. I'm a doctor, he would think, but I failed to save the person I loved most. And with soft compassion, he tended those who came to him.

He made house calls to grandmothers sitting up in bed, paisley head scarves tied under their chins. Listening to their chests and their complaints, he would write prescriptions and speak words of quiet comfort. They would grasp his hands. They would try to kiss them. And gently disentangling himself from their gratitude, he would promise to return soon.

The toothless old ladies recovered. Meeting one another in the street, they nodded in agreement. The heart-broken young doctor needed a wife. They sized up one another's daughters. And planning chance encounters at church, they cast willing daughters his way.

He took no notice. He had work to absorb him. He had Lidia, alive and dead. He had memory, guilt and grief. There was no room for love.

Chapter 4

When Ona heard that Juze was planning to move to the flat above Vytas' office, she thought the woman was crazy. Leaving the practicality of shared accommodation for the splendour of independent living was foolish. Life could take a turn for the worse, as it often did. Family had to stick together. And seeing them already as one family in one house, a handy arrangement in the event of children, she tried to forestall.

"We'll have to find new tenants," Ona said. Did this woman not know that they needed the income? Had this high-and-mighty mother-of-a-doctor suddenly forgotten the value of money?

"I'm sure you'll manage," Juze said, breaking the news with no small pleasure. She'd had enough of six people living in one small house. She'd had enough of these people. She wanted privacy and ease. She wanted to have their lives to themselves.

She gazed calmly at her landlady, enjoying the upper hand for once. She would meet her only at church. She would not have to keep her eye on Danguole. Vytas would be safe. She could stop watching and worrying.

One month, Ona thought. We have one month.

⁓

Vytas sat at his table, studying. Sensing Danguole in his doorway, he looked up. She hovered, holding her stomach and complaining of vague pain. She just wants to come in here, he thought, seeing her eyes darting past him into the room which he always took care to vacate when she cleaned. Quick to tell real sickness from false, he stepped out into the hallway.

"Let's go downstairs."

Her face fell.

"Where are your parents?" he said, glancing around the empty kitchen.

She shrugged.

He took her into the living room, sitting her down on the couch. Taking her pulse, he pronounced her likely to live. Just because I'm a doctor living in your house, he wanted to say, it doesn't mean you can do this. And smiling to himself at a ruse which had fooled no one, he prepared to go back upstairs.

She placed a hand on his sleeve.

"Doctor, would you teach me a little English? In those Eaton's sewing rooms where I work, it's Polish and Ukrainian all day long. The rest of the time, I help mother. Even if she would let me, there is no time for schooling. I so want to learn. Please, teach me a little?"

What a cocotte, Vytas thought. He did not like her touching him but did not want to be rude.

"How much English do you know?"

She released him, sitting up like an eager child on her first day at school. Clasping her hands in her lap, she recited name, address and telephone number, date and time. She's not stupid, he thought. Maybe she just needs a chance. And flattered by her deference, he found himself touched by her earnest desire to learn.

"As you can see, my English is not very good," she said, laughing.

He softened at her sweet way of making mistakes, as if putting herself down without really meaning it.

"Alright. A couple of lessons. On Sunday. After lunch. In the kitchen. We don't want to give our parents the wrong impression, do we?"

"Oh no, of course not," she said, lowering her lashes. "Thank you, Doctor, for helping a silly country girl."

He smiled at these clumsy but engaging attempts to ensnare. Poor girl, he thought. What harm could it do? After a few Sundays, they'd be gone.

⁂

The following Sunday, Juze watched with consternation as Vytas and Danguole sat at the kitchen table, heads together over an English grammar. Seeing Danguole leaning in close, following his finger down the page, consternation grew to dismay. There was hunger in the girl's every move. Vytas seemed blind. And hearing them settling into relaxed laughter, Juze's dismay turned to fear.

"Bruniuk, did you see that?" she said afterwards.

"Yes my love, but you must trust your son."

"I *do* trust *him*. It's *them* I don't trust."

The mother might be set upon a union but the father would see it was no good. He was sensible. He would see reason. It would be better discussed man to man.

"Would you speak to Jonas?" Juze said.

She burrowed into him, playing a dog seeking attention. She nudged him with her nose. She planted a kiss on his chin. Rubbing the stubble on his cheeks, she smiled up at him.

"Please?"

Brunius looked at the woman gazing up at him with affection, possibly even love. He remembered the desperation in her face when she first saw him, rather than her lover Alex, coming towards her on the station platform. Out of war's carnage, somehow, she had ended up his. It was still inexplicable. He would do anything she asked.

"Of course, my dear."

Brunius held her close. He understood little about the mysteries of love but knew it did not do the bidding of others. It could not be made to come or go. It landed wherever it wished. And encircling the most precious gift life had bestowed upon him, he promised to speak to Jonas.

⁕

One night after the others had gone to bed, Jonas and Brunius sat in the darkened kitchen. Passing the bottle back and forth, they poured rye into short stubby glasses. The thin handles were too delicate for their stocky fingers. The fluted skirting was too feminine to their eye. And surrounded by a silent house pretending to sleep, they remained quiet themselves.

Neither one knew how to start. Instead they spoke about the war.

"My mother wouldn't come with me," Jonas said pouring another drink. "I pleaded with her but she wouldn't leave the farm. She said they'd survived before and would survive again. It will pass, she said. My brothers and sisters stayed, too. They're probably dead. Or in prison. Or Siberia."

Years later he would learn that his mother and sisters had been shipped to Siberia. His sisters would survive to return home but his mother would not. She would lay buried far away in unfriendly foreign soil. His brothers would perish in prison. Grunting at the imponderable, he knocked back his drink.

Then, like a farmer at market, Jonas got down to business.

"So. What about these children of ours? My daughter. Your son."

Brunius, an old soldier, scratched his head.

"What do *you* think we should do?"

Their eyes met in the frank understanding of men talking only because their wives wished it. Two generals, their armies ranged up behind them, they had galloped out to the middle of the battlefield to see if hostilities could be averted. Brunius knew that he owed Juze loyalty. Jonas knew that Ona would make life hell if he came home without the doctor. Neither man knew how to prevent bloodshed.

"Let the youngsters figure it out for themselves," Jonas said.

"Yes, let them take care of themselves," Brunius said.

The men didn't mind whom their children married, only wishing them to be happy. Having discussed the matter, satisfied they could report back to their wives with clear consciences, they spoke about their lost country. Will we ever see it again? their eyes said, meeting once again. Will we ever go back? And in the darkened kitchen, they drank the last pure burning shots.

Juze stood in the bedroom, examining Vytas' striped brown and white shirt. Waving away Ona's offer of Danguole's services as a laundress, she had washed it herself by hand. Your daughter is not washing my son's clothes, Juze had thought. And suddenly sensing the girl hovering in the doorway, watching from behind, she turned to see a private knowing smile.

"What are you smiling about?"

"You'll find out soon enough."

Juze felt a slight alarm.

"Where's your mother?"

"Outside. She can't help you. There's nothing you can do. There's nothing anybody can do now." She leaned against the doorframe in languid contentment.

Dear God, Juze thought. The girl's pregnant.

"If you've done what I think you've done," she said, stepping forward and gripping the girl's arm, "then God help you."

"Don't touch me," Danguole said, lifting her arm free with exaggerated dignity. "You have to treat me with respect now."

Juze's heart plunged. How could this have happened? How could life turn out like this? This would never have happened Lithuania. They would be shackled to this family for life. And pushing past Danguole, she stormed out in search of Ona.

She found her in the garden, tending cucumber plants. Bending over, lifting the hairy vines, she untangled them. The thick succulent stalks broke easily. She worked with the knowledge of centuries. And reaching in between the large serrated leaves, she rearranged the plants upon on their mound of earth.

"So your daughter is pregnant," Juze said, hands on hips.

"Stupid girl," Ona said, stepping back to survey her work. "She's told you already."

So, the plan had been to say nothing until they knew for sure, an advantage which the girl, in her impatience to triumph, had given away. An ugly hope flashed across Juze's mind. Perhaps the girl would miscarry. She dismissed it with disgust. All life was good.

"She seduced my son. She trapped him."

"Oh I don't think so. From what she tells me, it was the other way around."

"Are you saying my son seduced her?"

Ona did not reply.

"What kind of marriage will it be, starting out like that?"

"Better than mine," Ona said.

There was a pause in hostilities.

"He doesn't love her."

"What of it? She's not a bad girl. She cooks, cleans and sews. She keeps house. She will take care of him and the children. My daughter's happiness for your son's reputation. Not a bad bargain."

Juze had a sudden glimpse of the woman's life as it must have been at home, an existence confined to the farm yard.

Within the daily drabness and toil, the marriage of a daughter would have been a shining star on the horizon. Maybe so, Juze thought, but they've trapped my son. They've trapped all of us. She shook off the unwelcome sympathy.

"She'll clean his office, too," Ona continued. "Of course, you would still be in charge. Danguole will listen to her mother and to her mother-in-law."

Checkmate, Juze thought.

She squinted through the clear June day. Their new lives, towards which they had been travelling, hovered in the distance. The vision seemed to wait and watch. Then it turned. And gliding away, rising over a hilltop, it sank out of sight on the other side.

Wait, Juze wanted to call out. Don't go. Don't leave us here.

"I will make a nice quiet wedding," Ona said. "Here. Among family. At home."

"No. My son will not hide in shame."

If it had to happen, it would happen in daylight. He may become your son-in-law, but he will never be yours. Never. I will make sure of that.

Ona shrugged her shoulders as if to say, Nice to have such money.

"We will have grandchildren, you and I," she added after a pause.

The child, Juze thought. She had forgotten the child. The present could not be changed but the future was not decided.

"*We* will name the child. No farm names. Something pretty. *Aušra*. Dawn."

Once again, Ona shrugged.

Ona plucked a curved cucumber, short, stubby and stout. Watching the farm woman running her thumb over its prickly bumps, Juze pondered the sour ironies of life. They had evaded dropping bombs. They had outwitted Russians and Germans. Falling for the oldest trick in the book, they had been bested by peasant cunning.

Chapter 5

Danguole stated that, not only would she have four bridesmaids, she wanted one hundred guests. Juze pointed out that few young women in their circumstances could afford a fancy dress for only one occasion. It's my wedding, Danguole said, tossing her head. No, it's not, Ona said. We are paying. In the end Danguole got two bridesmaids, fifty guests and no say.

The wedding took place on a Saturday at the unattractive hour of 9:00 a.m., the only time free in a city filled with exiles and a church calendar crowded with weddings, births and baptisms. Standing on the church steps in the cool September morning, the guests looked up at the clear blue sky. Everyone wanted everyone else to marry. Everyone wanted a home and children. Everyone longed for a happy return to normal life.

Every mother sitting in a church pew remarked on the good fortune of a farm girl catching a doctor. Pretending not to know the reason for the marriage, they watched the proceedings. Poor doctor, every mother thought, he could have done so much better with my girl. And lamenting the lost opportunity, eyeing every unmarried man in church, they turned their thoughts to the next likely prospect.

Vytas stood at the altar, steadfastly facing forward. Catching sight of his bride out of the corner of his eye, he saw a small woman in white. Lidia would understand, he thought. Surely she would understand and forgive. And waiting beside this unknown girl, he remembered a love that would never be replaced.

Danguole stood at the altar, resolutely facing forward. Wearing a plain-necked white dress she had made herself, she ignored her groom. She had been expecting a wedding necklace. None had come. And waiting tight-lipped at the altar, she gripped the bouquet of calla lilies to her waist.

The wedding luncheon took place at home, a long row of tables running from front window to back. Women nodded with approval at the thrift of tablecloths with edges overlapping, the mismatch of borrowed dishes, cutlery and glasses. The men noted the bottles of rye placed every few feet along the table. And dining on beef birds, chicken in mushroom sauce, poppy seed cake and the coveted *Napoleonas,* a wedding cake of twenty thin layers held together with custard and apricots, they praised food worthy of its reputation.

They toasted the bride, the groom, the bride's parents, the groom's parents, the bridesmaids and the ushers. Clinking spoons against glasses, they demanded a kiss from the bridal couple. They ate, drank and laughed. They gave speeches amid the wedding sparkle. And singing old songs about swains coming on steeds to woo maidens at the garden gate, they felt the stirring of tears.

If the well-wishers noticed the groom's stunned look, they attributed it to the momentous occasion. If he reached under the table for his bride's hand, they nodded at a newly married man's ardour. If the bride pulled her hand away, they approved her shyness. And attributing her pleased smile to the satisfaction of a woman well-married, his lost look to an excess of love, they sighed in contentment.

No one noticed the looks exchanged by the two mothers, one of triumphant contentment, the other of stolid resolve.

∽✺∾

After the wedding, Danguole wanted to move into Vytas' room upstairs. Playing with her baby, she would wait for her husband to come home. They would go downstairs for a dinner which her mother would have prepared. She might offer to clean up. And climbing back upstairs with husband and baby, she would go to bed.

"Vytas is moving downstairs," Ona said.

"No, he's not," Juze said. "We are all moving to the rooms above his office."

"My daughter is not going anywhere. She's pregnant. Who will take care of her? You? You'll be working as your son's secretary. If you and Brunius want to leave, I can't stop you but the newlyweds stay here."

"Then we stay, too."

"As you wish," Ona said. "Of course, now that you and Brunius are family, you will not be charged rent but we need the money from Vytas' room."

"They are a newly married couple. They need their privacy."

"Privacy? There'll be no privacy when the baby comes."

"It's the custom for the bride to move to the home of the groom," Juze said, exasperated beyond patience. "Danguole should move upstairs, it's only right."

"Never mind what's right. We'll do what's practical especially with a baby on the way. That shouldn't be too hard for a smart teacher woman to understand," Ona said, also exasperated beyond patience. Free lodging for two people. Did the woman have no head for practicalities? Could she not see the generosity of the gesture?

"So it'll be Vytas, Danguole and the baby in the same room as Jonas and you?"

"What's wrong with that? And who's going to look after the child while you are at work? Do you think my empty-headed daughter will be able to manage by herself? No. I'll have to help her. And on top of everything else I have to do. Be practical, Juze. There's no other way."

Juze glared at the floor, thwarted once again by this peasant woman.

"Oh don't worry, nothing's going to happen to your precious son," Ona said. "We'll take good care of him."

Vytas moved downstairs to keep the peace. His room was rented to a dark-haired man they rarely saw. The household now numbered seven. With the baby coming, it would soon be eight.

Ona took care of them all. She had meals ready on the table when they came home. She handed out lunches as they left in the mornings. Take it, she said, thrusting it into Juze's hands. Juze accepted. And a truce settled upon the household.

⁓

Every morning before leaving for the hospital, Vytas would go upstairs. Bending over his mother as she lay in bed, groggy with sleep, he would kiss her goodbye. She would roll over. She would touch his face. And tucking the blanket along the length of her spine as she fell back into the instant sweetness of sleep, he would think of his future child.

He would arrive at St. Joseph's, a brown brick building on the lake. Coming down Sunnyside Avenue, a narrow treed street along which visitors parked their cars, he would enter through Emergency. So much suffering, he would think, passing through the low-ceilinged waiting room filled with anxious relatives. And hurrying down the narrow tiled corridor, he would move towards work.

His patients were young and old, injured, unwell or simply fearful. Wearing his white coat, his stethoscope lying like two arms around his neck, he would attend. He would listen to their chests. He would soothe anguished faces. And sensing their fears abating, his pain would lessen, too.

At home, Danguole grumbled. As the pregnancy progressed, she grumbled that she didn't feel well. She grumbled that her husband spent too much time with his parents and not enough time with hers. She grumbled that he didn't like them. She accused him of not loving her. Calling him high and mighty, her reproaches were never ending.

He reasoned and reassured. Trying to mollify, he would cup her chin and turn her to face him. He would will his eyes to fill with the love she wanted to see. She would look back, cold and appraising. And knowing he could not make his wife happy, he would drop his hand and look away.

He found that it wasn't hard to spend all of his time working. Turning his mind away from his wife, her presence receded to the background, her voice no more bothersome than a distant radio. He spent little time at home. No one questioned him. And climbing the stairs to the darkened house late at night, anticipating the stiff chill of her back awaiting him in bed, his pang of guilt evaporated.

He would lift the covers, climbing in next to a woman who pretended that she hadn't heard him come home. Placing his arm around her, he would rest a hand on her burgeoning belly. He would try to believe that he might come to love her. He knew he could not. And lying in the dark, wishing that the woman next to him were Lidia, he dreamt of the life that should have been theirs.

On Christmas Eve Vytas arranged to be off duty. Wishing to atone for his shortcomings, he planned to spend the entire evening with his family. He would be attentive to his in-laws. He would show kindness to his unloved wife. And sitting amid family at the kitchen table, he took her unhappy hand in his.

Ona had prepared *Kūčias,* a meal served once a year. Cooking for two weeks, she had made herring in onions, herring in tomato sauce, herring in mushrooms, white fish balls, *vinegretas* and potato salad. She had baked a honey cake, a marble cake and *ausutes*, deep-fried twists of pastry dusted with icing sugar. She had spooned brandy over the Christmas cake in the basement. And going to the church, she brought home a communion wafer blessed by the priest.

She placed the opaque sleeve of wax paper on the table, unwrapping the *plotka* with reverence and care. Offering it in turn, she watched everyone break off a piece. Each person then offered his piece to another. They smiled with respect and good feeling. And watching the shared pieces growing ever smaller, Vytas felt the cohesion of family and tradition.

Part way through the meal, the phone rang.

"Don't answer it," Danguole said. "It'll just be the hospital. They can leave us alone for once."

"They might need me."

"And what about your own family?"

"What about the sick person who can't be at home with his family on Christmas Eve?"

"What has that got to do with me?"

He decided that he would go even if it wasn't necessary.

A woman had given birth in a taxi. She was running a slight fever. Could the doctor see her? He said he would come right away.

"Go," his mother said. "You are needed. We'll still be here when you come back."

"We'll see about that," Danguole snapped.

"And where will you be?" Ona said. "Sulking in the bedroom? Go then. When you want to come back, there might be no room for you. Be careful what you wish for, my girl."

Danguole turned away, sour and silent.

Vytas could stand no more. He got up. But the words stuck to him. What about your own family? He had no answer.

The night was cold and dark, the crisp snow crunching underfoot. Walking along the empty street to his car, he passed lit houses filled with families. They were celebrating closeness. He didn't mind. Alone in the silent night, thinking of Lydia, he found it beautiful.

The hospital was busy with Christmas Eve crises. He attended the young woman who had given birth. He checked on his other patients. He spent the night on duty. He didn't stop working. Nor did he wish to.

In the early morning, he looked in again on the new mother. Watching her sleep, he saw the flushed skin, the damp hairline lying dark along forehead, the half open mouth, the calm breathing after danger had passed. She opened her eyes with a groggy smile. She reached out a grateful hand. And grasping the living warmth, he held on.

Where are you, Lidia? Where are you, my love? Everywhere. Nowhere. Gone.

MARYTE

TORONTO

1950

When the commandant first came to her, she would not accept him. She wanted to bargain, to get something in return, something which mattered little to him but meant life-and-death to her. He was a gentleman and would not press. And eventually she would have to become his. But first she would negotiate safe passage for her brother.

Dobilas was not right in the mind. An idiot. The Nazis were shooting idiots.

What about you? the commandant had asked one night in bed, propped up on one elbow and looking down at this serious woman who seemed to care so little about herself.

Please. Safe passage for my brother.

But who will take care of you?

With the brother gone, the sister would lie heavy on the commandant's hands. And there were so many obliging women these days, refugees, needy and pretty, begging to be chosen. He was not unkind, but he knew himself well. He would tire of her. He promised to arrange passage for brother and sister both.

She had pressed her face against his chest, hiding genuine tears.

Chapter 1

Maryte hurried down Gore Vale Avenue, hunching her shoulders against the heavy snow. Moving between banks piled high on either side, she reached Queen Street. She turned right. She passed Shaw, Crawford, and Ossington. And approaching the mental hospital at 999 Queen she thought how lucky she was to be able to walk to work.

The street was an empty corridor filled with still-falling snow, a white world in which not even streetcars ran. Passing through a city brought to a standstill, she moved through silence. The peacefulness was comforting. It was like treasure. Ahead, the blurred yellow lights of the hospital beckoned.

She worked in the laundry, lifting heavy wet sheets out of washing machines into carts. Steadying the waterlogged mounds with one hand, she would push the rattling carts across the linoleum floor to the dryers. Sometimes the unwieldy mounds slithered to the floor. They had to be washed again. And picking them up, she was glad of the work after the listless life in the DP camp, even in such a sad place as this.

She would deliver the clean sheets, wheeling her trolley through to the wards. Moving along the hallways, she would see women muttering in front of walls, men shuffling in slippers, their half-open, green and grey striped bathrobes tied with a loose cord, their hairy legs naked. *Vargšai*, she thought. Poor souls. And thinking of her brother living at home with her, she knew these wretches to be worse off.

They had a rented room on the second floor of a house on Gore Vale Avenue. Returning home at the end of her shift, she would turn on the veranda to look at the winter park. Snow swirled across the white expanse of open ground in which earth and sky merged. A dull sun hung behind a distant trellis of black trees. And resting her gloved hands on the railing, her legs shielded by white panels with a raised diamond of green in the centre, she thought of tundra, bitter, empty and endless.

It could be Siberia, she thought. But it wasn't. It was Canada. And they were safe.

Dobilas would spend the day in their room, waiting for her to come home. While barley soup bubbled on the stove, he would lay out two bowls and two spoons on a table covered with a red checked cloth. He would turn to greet her, his lit face rounded like the back of a spoon. *Dobilai*, she would say, *Dobiluk*. And opening her arms wide she would step into golden light.

They were orphans, their mother having died giving birth to Dobilas, their father having hung himself soon afterwards. Some villagers said that the husband, having spirited the wife away over the objections of her family only to have her die, could not live with the guilt. Others said he was crazed with grief. Whichever it was, Maryte was eight years old and left with a baby brother.

She had found her father hanging from a rafter in the barn. She had watched the blacksmith gripping her father's body to cut it down, then the carpenter building a coffin for the second time. Why did you not live, papa? she thought, listening to the ringing of hammer and nails. Why did you not live for Dobilas and me? And watching her father's coffin being lowered into the ground, she saw husband being laid to rest beside wife.

There were no aunts or uncles to take them in. Their father's family shunned this wayward son whose passion made had him forget filial duty. Their mother chose not to speak of the faraway village from which she had been carried. Maryte didn't know her relations. She didn't know where to look. Finding themselves cast upon the benevolence of the villagers, they did well enough.

She learned to sew for the ladies of Vilnius, making dresses, embroidering tablecloths and pillowcases. Sitting on the front steps of the house that was now theirs, her work in her lap, she watched Dobilas romping in the field. She would take him on walks through the meadow. She would point out the names of flowers, trees and birds. And sitting on the front steps at dusk, a plate of bread and cheese on their knees, they would eat their evening meal.

She knew that something was wrong with him and that nothing could be done. Seeing the rapt expression he turned towards her, she knew they were closer than brother and sister. They were as close as husband and wife. They were parent and child. And taking care of him, she knew they would be bound forever.

When the war came they ran, carried along with the crowd, hiding from soldiers who would execute her idiot brother. In the DP camp the officials saw only Dobilas' sturdy body and strong capable hands. No one expected him to speak. No one could tell he was slow. And they were booked for passage to Canada.

They sought out a distant relation who had left before they were born. Finding him in a rooming house in Hamilton, they saw an old drunk, his undershirt sagging, his brown pants stained, his face covered with grey stubble, the stink of alcohol on his breath. Don't ask me for money, he said sweeping his arm over a room filled with nothing. And offering them Peak Freans from an open packet, he sent them on their way.

They walked from house to house looking for a room, their faces falling at the muttered word, *foreign.* Holding her brother's hand she glanced at his flat round face and bowl-cut blonde hair. Their parents were gone. How lucky they were to have one another. And glimpsing once again her parents' love, she understood how it might be harder to live than to die.

Maryte knew they were luckier still when they found Mrs. Moynahan. Hand on one hefty hip, the Irish woman's look was quick and understanding. Come on in, she had said opening the door wide. And reaching for their suitcase, she had taken them in.

They would sit on the front porch in summer, the three of them, Maryte, Dobilas and Mrs. Moynahan. Bringing out a cool pitcher of lemonade, Mrs. Moynahan would settle in to listen to their stories of escape. *No!* she would exclaim bringing a hand to her mouth. *You don't say.* And befriended by this benevolent woman who had kicked out her no-good drunk of a husband, Maryte knew just how lucky they were.

Sometimes she would remember the pull of her mother's

hand drawing her close, the stiff brush of her father's mous-
tache as he leaned into them. Whispering that soon she
might have a little brother, their eyes rested upon one another with delight and love. We will name him Dobilas, they
had said. Clover. For the sweet scented field in which he was
conceived. And heart aching, she would remember love.

She bent down in the hallway, removing the boots she had
received in the DP camp. Placing them on the newspaper,
she let her fingers linger on this luck which had arrived in
a parcel from Amerika. They were trim little boots, ankle
boots with laces. Fur trim ran along the top. And trying to
imagine a woman who would send off such stylish scarcely-
worn boots, she straightened to see Mrs. Moynahan waiting
in the kitchen doorway.

"There's been a little trouble," Mrs. Moynahan said,
arms crossed. "Dobilas used my bread. I had to go out for
more. In this snow. Look at me. My hair's a mess. And I have
company coming tonight."

Maryte looked past her landlady into the lit kitchen
beyond. A white tablecloth covered the black speckled For-
mica table with thick chrome legs. Two places were set, two
pretty rose flowered plates with rippled edges, and two wine
glasses. Mrs. Moynahan was entertaining.

"He just helped himself. He shouldn't do that. He
should stay out of my kitchen."

Maryte had impressed upon her brother never, *ever*, to
go into Mrs. Moynahan's kitchen. Going up and down the
stairs they might see their landlady sitting at her kitchen

table, leafing through a magazine and smoking a cigarette. She would wave. They would wave back. But she never invited them in and they never entered her part of the house.

"He wanted to feed the birds. He said they were hungry."

Maryte could see it now. Dobilas watching Mrs. Moynahan shovelling snow. Dobilas going downstairs to help. Dobilas passing Mrs. Moynahan's kitchen. His eye falling on the bread on the counter. His hand drawn by the shiny blue and white foil packaging. Dobilas rescuing the poor birds.

"Sorry Mrs. I tell him. I fix."

"Good. I'm happy to help you people but I have my limits."

Maryte looked again at the kitchen table set for two. First there would be muted laughter from behind the closed double-doors to the front room, then the clink of cutlery from the kitchen, then the silence from the bedroom. It was not Maryte's business. She pretended not to see.

"Well, no harm done. He did make me a sandwich first. He left it on the kitchen table for when I came in. It was very sweet actually. "

I am forgiven, Maryte thought, her chest releasing with relief.

Maryte did not understand the ways here, learning only too late from a cold look that she had transgressed. Waiting as Mrs. Moynahan hovered about to say more, she hoped for information. The moment passed. Having drawn the line between tenancy and friendship, Mrs. Moynahan became once again benevolent.

"Go on. Go on up to your brother. He's been waiting for you all day."

Maryte put her hand on the bannister, readying to mount

the stairs. Turning to her landlady in gratitude, she glanced again at the kitchen table. Two plates, two wine glasses. Two chairs waiting for occupants. And Mrs. Moynahan hoping for companionship and perhaps love.

⁓⁂⁓

Dobilas had stood at the second floor window, watching Mrs. Moynahan shovelling snow. She was nice, not like the two old people who looked after him when Maryte took the tablecloths to Vilnius. The widow Ponia Pauliene had lead pellet eyes and a shrivelled hand still strong enough to grip. Cranky Ponas Baliunas swiped at children with his cane, shouting at them to be quiet as they ran past. They were in Lithuania and far away.

Idiot. He knew that's what they called him. He was not as stupid as they thought. He knew for example that his mother had died while he was being born and that his father had hanged himself. He knew they were gone forever. He knew that Maryte was the only person he had in the world. He knew that she loved him and would always take care of him.

She told him their parents were in heaven but he was not fooled. He knew they were in the cemetery. When Maryte was in Vilnius and Ponia Pauliene's back was turned, testing her rising bread dough or smacking a grandchild sneaking a sip from the cherry syrup fermenting on the windowsill, he would slip away. He would go visit them.

Why did you leave, Mama and Papa, he would ask of the two dead people lying under the ground.

I had to leave, his mother would say.

And I had to go with her, his father said.

Maryte was always talking about how their parents were waiting for them in heaven but he didn't believe it. They were not living in another world where he would see them again. They were dead. They would stay dead. But not wanting to upset her, he said nothing.

Mrs. Moynahan was sending the snow flying with brisk vigorous strokes. Wearing her husband's old parka, she looked like a babushka. You're going to leave me something even if it's only this coat, you old sod, she had said, telling Dobilas and Maryte the story with a laugh. But putting her arms into the sleeves of the capacious brown coat, she would pull it close and inhale the smell.

Once, Ponas Baliunas and Ponia Pauliene had come upon him playing in the meadow. They stopped to watch, leaning on a bridge over a brook. They prodded one another. They laughed. And he had heard both their laughter and their words.

Look at that idiot, the old man had said.

A happy idiot, the widow had said.

Arms flung wide, head thrown back, Dobilas spun in the sunshine. Dropping onto his back, he looked at the flower stalks rising up either side of his face. Isn't it lovely to be a flower? he whispered. Do you like being a flower in the sun? And chest rising and falling in gentle contentment, he hummed to himself in shut-eyed bliss.

He's having a fit, the old man said.

Who knows what's going on in his mind, the widow said.

Dobilas glanced towards the old couple as he rose, brushing the leaves and twigs from his trousers. Smacking himself

on the back to dislodge any remaining debris, he began twirling again. With a shout he dropped onto his back. He lifted
his arms and legs in the air and waggled them. Sticking out
his tongue, he lolled his head from side to side.

What's the idiot doing now? the old man said.

Heaven knows, the widow said. He's not right in the
mind, poor boy.

They tottered off, the old man tapping his way back to
the village, the old widow leaning on his arm.

Mrs. Moynahan was tossing salt on the sidewalk from
a heavy bag held in her arms. Grappling with the shifting
bag, she struggled to keep it from spilling. Her face grew red.
Her hair straggled out from beneath her parka hood. Going
down to help, he heard Maryte's words in his head.

Don't go into Mrs. Moynahan's kitchen. She lives down
there. We live up here.

He could make her a sandwich. She might tell him to
make one for himself. She might invite him to sit down.
They might eat together just like Maryte and him.

The kitchen cupboards were plywood, flat and plain.
Tucking his fingers under the cupped metal handle of a
drawer, he almost pulled it open. An oblong mirror hung
over the sink. Why did she have a mirror over the kitchen
sink? Dobilas thought. And imagining her sneaking looks in
the mirror while she washed the dishes, he turned away.

He made a bologna sandwich just as she liked it, with
mustard and a pickle on the side. Placing the plate on the
table, the pickle set well away from the bread so that the
juices wouldn't seep, he decided not to make one for himself. He did not like the bland smoothness of bologna. He
liked the chunky zest of *kielbassa*. And leaving the sandwich

on the table for Mrs. Moynahan, he stepped towards the back window and looked out.

The world was white, the wheelbarrow a soft mound covered in snow. Sparrows clung to the rippled black wire fence, their feathers fluffed against the cold, their heads tucked into themselves. They had nothing to eat. He and Maryte had been without food during the war. If no one had helped them, they would have died.

The bread package lay open on the counter. Mrs. Moynahan's sandwich was ready on the table. She was taken care of. Now he could help the birds. And picking up the soft white bread he slipped outside.

∽≈∾

"Dobiluk," Maryte called coming up the stairs. "Dobiluk, where are you?"

"Maryte!" he cried leaning over the railing. Clattering down the stairs, he threw his arms around her.

She let him burrow into her, rubbing his face against her chest. Ponia Pauliene might have scolded him for wasting bread on birds but nothing more. Let them fend for themselves, she would have said. In this new world where he understood even less than her, he had no idea that he'd done anything wrong or that anyone might be mad at him.

"You must not touch Mrs. Moynahan's bread," she said, wagging her finger with mock severity. "Do not go into her kitchen. Stay here. Wait for me to come home."

Dobilas nodded, his smile vanishing.

Maryte wondered if he really understood. At times he seemed to, at other times not. She would repeat over and over just to be sure. She did so now. Dobilas listened until she was finished.

"*Vakarienė*," he said. Supper. And there was magic in the word.

Moving into deft action he set out dinner. He ladled out deep red borscht thick with shredded beets. He placed soft meat dumplings on their plates along with plain boiled potatoes. They had no dessert. Cakes were reserved for the weekend when Maryte had time to bake.

"Come," she said after they had eaten. "Bring your picture book."

Dobilas fetched the book of fairy tales brought from Lithuania. Settling against her, he listened to stories. Old couples conversed with roosters and hens. Princesses with long flaxen braids had ten brothers. Witches dragged young maidens into the lake. Swans and ravens spoke with human voices. Aglow with delight, he heard stories filled with magic and love and fright. And turning the page Maryte read about how the hare came to have a split lip:

> One day, a goose encountered a hare.
>
> Why are you so downcast? said the goose.
>
> No one fears me, said the hare. I'm going to drown myself.
>
> Don't be silly, said the goose. If you wish to be feared, hide in the bushes. When the sheep come by, leap out. You will see. They'll be frightened.
>
> The hare did as the goose said. He hid in a bush. He waited for sheep. When they came, he leapt out. And it was just as the goose said. They were frightened and ran away.

> *Overjoyed, the hare started laughing. And laughing and laughing, he split his lip.*

Dobilas murmured, head resting on her shoulder. Leading him along in half-sleep, leaning over him, she put him to bed. His eyes flew open. He smiled without seeing her then dropped back to sleep. And tucking the covers in more tightly, she returned to the book:

> *Elenyte and Jonukas, an orphaned brother and sister, left home to seek their fortune. On the road they came upon a horse's footprint filled with water.*
>
> *Jonukas leant down to drink.*
>
> *Don't drink, dear brother, Elenyte said, you will turn into a foal.*
>
> *Further down the road they came upon an oxen's footprint filled with water.*
>
> *Jonukas leant once more to drink.*
>
> *Don't drink, Elenyte said. You will turn into an ox.*
>
> *Further still they came upon a ram's footprint filled with water.*
>
> *This time Jonukas stooped and drank.*
>
> *He turned into a lamb. And Elenyte continued, leading her brother on a rope.*
>
> *A king found the beautiful young girl and her lamb asleep in a rick. Learning that she was an orphan, he resolved to raise her. So the orphaned sister and brother came to live in the castle of a king.*
>
> *One day the king decided to have the lamb slaughtered.*
>
> *It is my brother, the young girl cried, begging him not to do it.*

And the king relented.

Elenyte grew into a beautiful young woman whom the king married. A witch, eaten by envy and wishing the king for herself, resolved to do the young woman in.

The witch pushed Elenyte into the lake. The girl became a golden carp. The witch stole her clothes and returned, disguised, to the king.

How that lamb disgusts me! the witch declared as she lay in the king's bed. For love of god, please have him slaughtered.

What ravings are these? said the king. You wish to slaughter the brother whom you love?

Do you think a lamb could really be my brother? the witch said. I am ill. If I don't have lamb meat, I will surely die.

The king was filled with pity for the lamb. Wondering how his loving wife could think of eating its flesh, he refused to have it slaughtered.

The lamb knew that the witch wished to kill him. He trotted to the edge of the lake. He sang out over the waters—

> *Elenyte, my sister, Elenyte, Elenyte*
> *The master will slaughter me,*
> *The servants are sharpening their knives,*
> *The maidens are washing the platters*
> *The witch covets my flesh.*

From the lake his sister called back:

> *My brother lamb, my little lamb, little lamb*
> *Tell my master, the king*

> *Let him call together the villagers*
> *Let them weave a silken net*
> *Let them catch the golden carp*

The servants raced to tell the king that they had heard a singing lamb being answered by a singing fish.

The next morning, the king hid at the lake's edge.

Once again the lamb sang out to his sister. Once again she replied.

The king returned to his castle. He summoned his villagers. He directed them to weave a silken net. And they caught the golden carp.

They pulled the carp from the water. The fish became once again a woman. The lamb became once again a man. And the king recognized his true wife.

He ordered the witch killed.

And Elenyte and Jonukas lived happily ever after with the king in the castle.

Chapter 2

When Mrs. Moynahan opened the front door, Steponas saw the leap of interest in her eyes. Letting her gaze linger, the russet-haired woman in a silk turquoise robe took him in bit by bit. Her robust Canadian body would be firm, white and smooth. She would give as good as she would get. And his interest leapt too at the prospect of pursuit and possible capture.

"Maryte never told me you were such a handsome devil," she said, pleasure scudding across her face like wind ruffling the surface of the sea.

He followed her upstairs, watching the solid buttocks shifting under the silk. Surveying the room, noticing only the bed where he would sleep, he paid her scant attention. He felt her eyes upon him. It had always been thus. And after the war, women were drawn to the deprivation pulsing off him like heat.

"It's a back bedroom," she said. "Dobilas and Maryte face the street."

He nodded but said nothing. Looking around, he pretended to consider.

"They cook their own meals. You can take yours in the kitchen with me."

He turned to her, his gaze full and direct.

"Bedroom eyes," she murmured.

She was bold this Canadian, bolder than any Lithuanian or German girls he had known.

"Okay. I take."

He could almost see her going weak at the knees.

"Dinner isn't until six," she said, "but come downstairs if you're hungry. I'll make you a little snack if you like."

"I wait for dinner."

"Cheeky bugger," she said with a curling smile before going downstairs.

Steponas stretched out on the bed, hands behind his head, legs crossed at the ankles. Already he could imagine lifting himself off her white bulk after love. She would reach up to keep him close. She would soothe and assuage. He didn't mind being rescued for a time.

He looked at his watch. Six o'clock. He would not go downstairs yet.

Swinging his legs over the side of the bed, he pulled his tan leather briefcase towards him. Carried from Lithuania and always kept close, it held his documents. A soft green notebook, a diary stared on the day he left and no longer kept. The truck-driving licence earned in the American sector working for the army. The identification card for his ten-month contract in the gold mines in Central Patricia. And his certificate of admittance to Canada. They were his only credentials. Then putting the papers away, he fell once more to musing about women.

They liked to tease and invite, playing hard-to-get or making forthright advances. More than seduction they wanted love, especially the lonely ones like Mrs. Moynahan who pretended not to be. Moira, he would say, My Moira. It was so easy to murmur endearments and bestow caresses, easy to give them what they wanted, to make them happy for a time.

He looked at his watch. Six fifteen. He would go downstairs and begin the seduction of a woman who wore a turquoise silk robe in the afternoon, a robe with an embroidered peacock on the back, a gold and silver peacock spreading its tail. She knew how to spoil herself. And she would spoil her man. Sensing the pleasure to be had, he decided to stay for a while.

***

Steponas would lie on his bed after dinner, his door ajar. He would watch Mrs. Moynahan saunter past on her way to her evening bath. He liked seeing the thin turquoise silk against firm flesh and hearing the slap slap of her satin slippers against naked heels. He wanted her to see him. And he liked the feeling that at a moment's notice he could push the door open.

He knew that she saw him, that she was feigning indifference, her head lifted and turned away. Who did she think she was fooling? Perhaps herself. Well he would wait.

He heard the drum of rushing water in the next room and imagined her disrobing. She would admire her breasts and buttocks in the mirror. Sinking into the hot water with sighing pleasure, she would splash about. She would soap her breasts. She would rinse herself and rise out of the water like a Venus. She would rub herself down briskly. Flushed, she would walk back to her bedroom, damp patches of turquoise silk stuck to her skin.

He must wait. He must await an invitation. And one evening, passing on her way back to her room, she cast him a swift glance. He visited her that night.

Her room was so blindingly white that, for a moment, Steponas couldn't see. Waiting for his vision to clear, he discerned a white armchair set upon a white shag rug, a white dressing table covered with women's trinkets of cut glass. Mrs. Moynahan lay upon a white bed like a goddess, her russet hair on glorious display. She lifted her arms to receive him. And moving towards her, he fell into the downy whiteness of a snowstorm.

Afterwards he asked politely if he could leave the door slightly open.

"Oh no, love," she said. "I couldn't do that."

He visited only at her invitation. Never taking the first step, asking only with his eyes as she passed on her way to the bath, he would wait to see if she wished company. If she nodded, he would lie back on his bed. Hands clasped behind his head, he would anticipate the pleasure of love. It was the closest he came to feeling happy.

Steponas never talked to women about himself or his past but, if he was in the mood, he would tell Mrs. Moynahan bits that he thought she might understand. He had lived in a house by a forest. His father had been a woodsman. He was probably dead now. His mother had died long ago.

"Oh my darling," Mrs. Moynahan said, reaching a hand up his face.

He caught her hand, stopping it. He did not like to be touched in that way.

"Beautiful," he murmured, turning it over and kissing the palm.

She leant back, a smile of deep satisfaction on her face. In the pure whiteness of the room, atop the white body, inside the oblivion of a snowstorm, he made love to her again.

He did not tell her that his drunken father used to beat him until he grew big enough to hit back. He did not say that Germans had surrounded churches on Sunday mornings, snatching up young men for the Russian front. He did not say that he had hidden on a barge plying up and down the Nemunas River. He did not tell her that he had slipped back to see his father. He did not describe their last conversation, the words driven into his skull like nails.

"Go then, if you want," his father had spat across the kitchen table, slumped in the gloom of drink and a doomed future. "It will be no loss to me."

"Fend for yourself then," Steponas had said. And yet he could not just leave an old man who could be dead soon, if not from war then from drink.

"Father. Come with me. Please. Together we will manage."

His father had raised his head, shaking it like a surly bear.

"No! I will never leave my country. If you want to go, you snivelling puppy, then go. I will fight to the end. I will die fighting."

And he'd brought his fist down on the table.

Steponas took a last look at the room in which he had lived his entire nineteen years. He saw his mother cowering behind the green ceramic stove, felt her shoving him out the way of his father's blows. There was no reason to stay. He could carry with him anything worth remembering. And visiting his mother's grave to ask forgiveness, he left.

Chapter 3

⟿⟍⟍⟍⟍⟍

Every Sunday, Maryte took Dobilas to mass at the Lithuanian church, a modest building at the corner of Dundas and Gore Vale. In the small chapel rather like a low-ceilinged extension off to one side, she would pray to the Virgin Mary, her blue-robed head surrounded by a starburst of gilt. God could be of more practical help, Maryte would say to the ornate icon. But rising from her knees, she always felt calmed, uplifted and refreshed.

They would drift west along Dundas among parishioners heading towards Lithuania House and a good lunch. Sitting at round tables for ten, they would eat soft beef patties or potato pudding topped with sour cream and fried bacon bits. They would trade news. They would gossip and laugh. Then fortified by friends and food and good cheer, they would return home.

They would turn down Crawford Street towards Queen, walking past pretty houses, narrow and tall. Approaching the mental hospital, she would draw her brother closer. She did not want him to see the poor souls living there. She did not want him going near. And steering him off the street, they would enter the sanctuary of the park.

They would walk beside a row of tall balsam trees, moving as if behind a line of soldiers holding guns. Passing behind their backs, moving through protection, they would emerge into the open heart of the park. They would step off the path into the freedom of the grass. They would walk through the memory of their meadow back home. And imagining the soldiers gunless, their palms holding aloft the canopy of leaves, she knew it would never happen.

Their landlady would be sitting on the front porch, leafing through her women's magazine. Lifting her head, she would greet them with a friendly wave. Her smile would be slightly rueful. Brother and sister walking together, she would murmur. And jesting, she would say that a husband was needed.

Maryte didn't mind. She had Dobilas. She had work. She had a place to live and a good landlady. And she had this little patch of earth.

One Sunday afternoon Maryte turned to see Mrs. Moynahan standing in their doorway. Maryte never ventured into her landlady's domain, always leaving the rent on the little hall table. Mrs. Moynahan came upstairs only to use the bathroom. Their friendly co-existence relied upon a mutual respect for distance. Now their landlady stood in the doorway, a look of friendly interest on her face.

"Could we talk? Just us girls?"

Mrs. Moynahan wanted to talk to her? Perhaps she had boyfriend trouble.

Maryte hurried to the sink, filling the kettle. Setting

cups and plates on the table by the window, she gave Mrs. Moynahan the rose plate and herself the cup with the chipped lip. She put out an apple torte freshly baked. She sent Dobilas to the park. They would be two women together discussing womanly things.

Mrs. Moynahan sat down, lifting her face to the sun. Her complexion was clear as glass, its perfection effortless. Maryte did not begrudge the natural advantages that eased life in small ways. Attractiveness could also bring unwanted attentions. And settling down across from Mrs. Moynahan, she offered her a thick piece of apple cake.

"Don't mind if I do," Mrs. Moynahan said. "Got to watch my weight, though."

What a problem, Maryte thought, having so much to eat that weight was a worry.

She and Dobilas still ate as they had during the last winter of the war and the four years in the DP camp. Unable to get rid of the fear that tomorrow there would be no food, they ate slowly and carefully. They tasted every morsel. They waste nothing. Sweeping crumbs into their hands, they licked their palms.

Mrs. Moynahan's pink tongue flicked at the corners of her mouth. Moistening her finger, she lifted the crumbs left on her plate. She sipped delicately from a cup. She dabbed at the corners of her mouth with her napkin. Then waving away offers of more cake, more tea, she leaned back with a satisfied sigh.

"We have to do something about your appearance. Otherwise, how are you going to get a man?"

Maryte looked down at her grey wool sweater buttoned along its length, her straight dark skirt falling well below her knees, her comfortable black laced oxfords. Sewing for the fine ladies of Vilnius, she had learned to remain invisible, the touch that pinned and tucked. She had no money for fabric. She wore what she was given or came across. She had no interest in her appearance or in men.

"First things first," Mrs. Moynahan said, getting down to business. "That hair has to go."

No! Maryte thought, her hand flying up to her hair.

Every morning she braided it, her dreamy fingers moving down the length of hair. Every evening Dobilas brushed it out, the strokes pulling her head pleasantly back. Her father had done the same for her mother. She loved the remembered rhythm and the touch. She shrunk from anyone touching it, even the well-meaning Mrs. Moynahan.

"No offense," Mrs. Moynahan said, taking command, "but you look like a little old lady."

Maryte did not wish to offend. Submitting like a child to a mother's hand, she let Mrs. Moynahan brush, pin and spray. She could put her hair back into braids afterwards.

"Pucker up," Mrs. Moynahan said, swivelling open a tube of lipstick.

Maryte obliged. She never wore lipstick. In the laundry, sweat ran freely. Lipstick would not stay put. She could explain that.

"Now I'm going to get something from downstairs. In the meantime you get out of those drab things."

Undress in front of Mrs. Moynahan?

Maryte's hand went to the white bra strap mended with black thread. It didn't matter in front of farm women who wore thick sweaters and boots or refugees who had only the clothes in which they had left home. No doubt Mrs.

Moynahan wore peachy satin underwear next to her flaw-
less skin. Mrs. Moynahan, a Canadian woman with dresses
such as the one with which she now returned.

The dress was red and white polka dots with a tight
fitting halter top and a circle skirt cinched by a wide belt of
white patent leather. She had never made such a dress. She
had never seen such a dress. It was a dress for women who
could afford to give away such things, women who had sent
parcels overseas to refugees in DP camps. Women like Mrs.
Moynahan. It was not for her.

"Put it on," Mrs. Moynahan said. "Go on. I can't get into
it anymore but it'll fit you."

Maryte could see that she must.

"Was I ever right," her landlady said, zipping her up and
turning her around. "Now these." And she brandished a pair
of red high-heeled peep-toe shoes.

How was Maryte supposed to walk in those?

She was on her feet all day long. When she got home,
she just wanted to put them up. She would never wear such
shoes. She hoped they wouldn't fit. Unfortunately, they fit
perfectly.

"You could use a pedicure," Mrs. Moynahan said.

Pedicure? What folly was this? Polish would chip inside
her shoes as she walked between washers and dryers. What
vanity and idleness. What a waste of money. Maryte stared
down at her feet and said nothing.

"And you need to shave those legs."

Shave her legs? Maryte had never done such a thing.

"Time to look at yourself," Mrs. Moynahan said, placing
her in front of the bathroom mirror.

Maryte looked at the red and white polka dot dress, the

red peep-toed shoes, the red lipstick and the teased hair. This was a woman who would go out dancing in a swirl of skirts, a pampered idle woman who had nothing better to do than to think of such things. It was not the woman she was. It was not a woman she wanted to be. She knew better than to think of this as a possibility for herself.

"Now that's going to get a man's attention," Mrs. Moynahan said. "We just have to get you out there. Show you around a bit. Maybe go to a dance. The men will lap you up."

"No!" Maryte cried. "I no go with men."

Maryte saw the pleasure ebbing from her landlady's face. She had not meant to imply that *Mrs. Moynahan* went with men, only that she herself didn't. No, that wasn't right either. She didn't know how to explain it. Mrs. Moynahan withdrew, becoming cool and aloof.

"It's hard to find a man and god knows you sure could use one but far be it from me to tell you how to live your life," she said with a shrug.

Now Maryte knew that she had truly offended. Mrs. Moynahan would no longer have them in the house. She would throw them out. They would have to start all over again. Eyes filling with tears, she stood mute and miserable.

"There there," Mrs. Moynahan said, patting her arm. "Life's not so bad, is it?"

Life was not so bad but how could she explain the aches layered upon her soul. The loss of her parents, an ache brought from home. The bargain struck with the commandant, an ache collected along the way. The ache of new life here with its constant need for carefulness, its lack of comfort and ease. There was too much to tell. Nor could she explain, not even to the kindly Mrs. Moynahan.

"Never mind dear," Mrs. Moynahan said. "No harm done."

Maryte looked at herself in the mirror once again after Mrs. Moynahan was gone. Such a dress, such hair, such shoes were not for her. She was used to humbler circumstances both in attire and in life. She could not become what the helpful Mrs. Moynahan wanted. It was not the kind of help that was needed.

Maryte took her new appearance on an outing, more for Mrs. Moynahan's sake than for her own. Walking through the soft spring air, she practised her request. Please I borrow book? She entered the library in her crisp new dress and beehive hairdo. Her high heels clicked on the tile floor. And approaching the front desk, she felt that at least she looked right.

Men and women sat at long oak tables, reading by lamps with green glass shades. Quietly turning pages, they read in private concentration. Soon she would join them. She would ask for a grammar book to improve her English and for a novel to learn how to live here. But first she would need a library card.

The librarian was a stylish pretty blonde in an elegant summer suit of light grey check. A white silk scarf ran the length of her neck, tucked along the rim of the shawl collar. She carried herself in the manner of one accustomed to being considered. She looked up. Her dark eyes contained a lack of friendliness.

"Yes?"

"Please, library cart?" Maryte said.

"Cart? What do you mean cart?" A furl of distaste formed along her perfectly lipsticked mouth. "Oh, you mean *card*. Well, I can't imagine why you would want one. You can't even speak proper English. What ever would you do with a book?" And lowering her head, she returned to ticking off returned books.

Maryte looked at the readers, wishing that one would rise from their table and come over. Putting a comforting arm around her shoulders, they might tell her that it didn't matter. She would soon learn. She would not be judged for what she couldn't know. And turning quietly, leaving the land of the polished, educated and well-dressed, she returned to the world that she knew.

Chapter 4

There were no secrets in a small house. Maryte would encounter Steponas returning to his room as she went to the bathroom in the early morning. Mrs. Moynahan would chat over the fence to her neighbour Mrs. Carlilse. Steponas would hint to his compatriots that he was getting more than just room and board. Now that he had bedded his landlady, everyone knew.

With a gallant sweeping bow, he would offer Maryte first use of the bathroom. Passing close by him in the intimacy of the narrow hallway, she wanted to place a hand on his arm. Be careful, she wanted to say. You will only end up in trouble. And raising his eyebrows as if reading her thoughts, he would smile in mischievous collusion.

Maryte would lie in bed at night, knowing such pleasure could not be hers. Listening to the moans of lovemaking rising up from the room below, she would imagine Mrs. Moynahan's white body lying beached and limp, Steponas stretched out beside her in satisfaction. She could sense their private love talk. She could hear Steponas returning to his room. And she would hear the creak of springs as he climbed into his own bed and the silence of his peaceful sleep.

She lay in bed, listening and imagining.

In his bed, Dobilas listened and imagined, too.

Dobilas sat on the front porch in the sweet summer heat, looking at the park across the street. Gazing into the dense dark green, he breathed in the beauty of the world. The happy summer songs of birds surrounded him. A white sun hung in the hazy sky. Settling himself doglike, chin upon paws, he waited for Maryte's return.

Mrs. Moynahan dozed in the chair beside him, head tipped back in the heat, magazine fallen to her lap. Her square-necked sleeveless coral blouse exposed the summer freckles which she so disliked. He would lick his thumb and rub them away. She would laugh and smile at him then. Moving her lips in a gentle muttering, she woke up with a soft little snort.

"What are you looking at?' she said, picking up her magazine. "Is your sister doing anything about getting you a job? You can't just hang around here all day long. I'm not a baby-sitter. I can help you people out now and again but you have to work."

He looked at her, eyes wide with surprise. This was not the friendly Mrs. Moynahan whose breasts lay like balloons beneath the coral fabric. He wanted to lay his head against them. He wanted to have his hair stroked. He walked his fingers along the railing in her direction.

"Stop playing silly buggers," she said, eyeing his moving hand.

He inched his fingers forwards.

"Stop that," she said, smacking his hand with the magazine. "You're not that dumb."

He reached out. He placed a hand on her breast and shut his eyes. Soft as pillows.

"You pig! You dirty filthy pig!"

She leapt up. She slapped his face hard. She stormed into the house. The screen door banged shut behind her.

He placed one hand to his stinging cheek, tears springing to his eyes. The birdsong sounded harsh and shrill, the feathery little creatures leaning forward, their sinewy talons gripping the branches, their sharp beaks open, their yellow and black throats pulsing. Idiot, they jeered. Stupid, stupid idiot. His heart, cresting at the world's beauty, fell.

He went inside to the small back bedroom upstairs, the vacant room with the single bed, dresser and window. Stepping into the plainness of the unoccupied room, he discovered a grey curtain and behind it a cupboard, large, empty and deep. Shelves lined three walls. A clothes rod ran along the rim. A person would have to scrabble in on his knees to reach what he wanted.

He climbed in, turned around and sat down. Facing out into the room, he drew the curtain. Daylight filtered through the thin grey fabric. Bold brightness lit the striations in the weave. And sitting cross-legged in the dimness of his cave, he watched the strips of gleaming light.

꙰

While she worked, Maryte would think about her parents. Rolling her metal cart over the concrete floor, she remembered her mother's kiss on the top of her head, her father's proud smile. It was hard to be without them. She wished she could see them again. She would speak to them, tell them she loved them and show them that she and Dobilas were alright.

She walked home along streets where her parents had never lived. Wishing she could see her father standing on the corner, talking business with a neighbour while her mother chatted to the wife, she would welcome their ghosts. She stopped to look up into the trees. The leaves rustled peacefully. One day she and Dobilas would return to the land that held their parents' presence.

Mrs. Moynahan was waiting in the lit kitchen doorway at the end of the hallway. Looking Maryte up and down, there was distaste in her manner and voice. Dobilas had tried to take advantage of her. He had tried to force himself upon her. Luckily she had been able to fend him off.

Maryte had to stifle a giggle at a bumbling Dobilas overpowering the mighty Mrs. Moynahan. In their village such attentions would have been received with a sharp, good natured smack. The story would be passed around, a joke told at farm weddings. No harm done, the villagers would have said. Just a curious idiot boy. But their landlady was no farm girl and this was not Lithuania.

"I tell him no good," Maryte said.

"Not good enough. I want you out of here."

Maryte's heart leapt with fear. This was too harsh a punishment. Dobilas didn't know the difference between right and wrong. His action didn't mean anything. It certainly didn't mean what Mrs. Moynahan was implying.

"Mrs. Moynahan, please."

"You can have a few days to find a new place but I'm sorry, you have to go."

To Maryte, the woman didn't seem sorry at all.

"Please," she said, fear growing to alarm, "he no bother you again, I promise."

"I don't see how you can rightly guarantee that. He shouldn't be on the loose. In fact, he should be locked away. In the loony bin. That's where he belongs. 999 Queen. And that's where he'll end up if he doesn't watch his step."

Maryte was pitched into panic.

"Please, Mrs. Moynahan. We no make trouble. We go."

Mrs. Moynahan sniffed. "You have to be gone by Saturday. In the meantime, keep that pervert out of my sight. He's a menace to women. He'd better stay out of my way if he knows what's good for him."

Afraid of being kicked out then and there, Maryte suppressed a rising anger. Where was the kindly woman who taken them in, the friendly woman who had offered advice on dresses, hair and shoes, the understanding woman with whom they had shared lemonade and stories? Mrs. Moynahan, understanding no more. She seemed a different person. Flushed and upset, Maryte went upstairs to look for her naughty brother.

She stood in the hallway, listening to the exaggerated scuffling coming from the guest bedroom at the end of the hallway. Going into their room instead, she moved chairs back and forth, opened and shut the closet door. She played hide-and seek. She calmed herself. And gentling her voice, she called out in sing-song as she went down the hall.

"Where's my Dobilas? Where could he be? I know! I know where he is! And I'm coming to get him!"

Maryte stepped into the small back bedroom which Mrs. Moynahan kept unrented in case her brother came from Ireland for a visit. Seeing the single bed neatly made, the bureau kept dusted and uncluttered, the clean curtains opened onto the sunny outdoors, she felt the emptiness of a room to which a brother never came. Mrs. Moynahan had only lodgers and lovers. She had no one who mattered. And standing before the cupboard in which Dobilas hid, Maryte watched the curtain swaying slightly with his breath.

"Dobiluk, are you in there?"

A giggle came from behind the curtain.

"Dobiluk, come out."

He scuttled further back inside the cupboard.

"Dobiluk. Come out now. Please."

She bent her head in patience, waiting at the curtain. Thrusting out his hand and climbing down, he came into her arms. I must get him away from her, she thought as he rubbed his grinning face against her chest. It is no longer safe here.

Chapter 5

Maryte hovered in her bedroom doorway, waiting for Steponas to pass. Intercepting him on his way back to his room after dinner, she asked to speak to him. She invited him to step into her room. She closed the door quietly with both hands. And leading him to the table by the window and lowering herself into the chair opposite, she described the day's events.

"You'd like me to speak with Mrs. Moynahan," he said.

Maryte looked down at her hands, grateful not to have to ask.

"She's stubborn. She might not listen," he said

But you are a man, Maryte thought. And her lover.

"Perhaps she will listen to you. You are closer to her."

He gave her a swift look, his expression cocky and amused.

Her eyes flitted over the contours of his chest. How she wanted to rest her hands upon it, to lay her head against its lovely undulating landscape. Help me, she wanted to say. Tell me everything will be alright. And feeling him soften, she understood that he had agreed.

Steponas returned to his room, shutting the door behind him. Thinking of Maryte's slumped, dumpy figure, pitying the earnest beseeching look, he had almost held her. It would not do to become entangled. He did not wish to lead her on. It would not be right to raise the hopes of this good woman who was already an old maid.

He lay on his bed, listening to the clank of pots and pans rising from the kitchen below. Feeling a sudden stab of loneliness, he turned away. It was no good to get attached. Mrs. Moynahan was okay for now. And there were plenty of pretty young Lithuanian girls gathered in this city, far more than he would have encountered back home.

He had become enamoured of such a girl once, a maid in this mother's kitchen, a girl who had shyly returned his glances. Giving the girl a good scolding, his mother next turned to him. Marry upwards, she had said. And respecting her wisdom, he left off with the girl with the sweetly pointed chin.

He thought of his mother standing at the stove, stirring a pot. Playing on the floor at her feet, stirring an empty bowl with a wooden spoon, he had recited his prayers. She had corrected him when he got it wrong, guided him when he got stuck. Her manner had been calm, loving and gentle. And thinking of his landlady, a spasm of irritation passed through him at this hysterical Canadian woman.

Mrs. Moynahan would be just as unkind to him one day. Knowing how to gauge danger, he always left before getting hurt. War had only sharpened his senses. It was time to move on. And resting on his bed, arms behind his head, he decided not to visit his landlady tonight.

Steponas watched without comment as Mrs. Moynahan served dinner the following evening. Removing a casserole from the oven, she banged the door shut with her knee. She slopped two spoonsful onto his plate. She smacked it down in front of him. Ignoring her, he ate while she sat glowering at him across the table.

"You didn't come last night," she said. "Why not? Not in the mood?"

Not in the mood for you, he thought.

"Answer me," she said.

He pushed his plate away, having no taste for tomato soup from a tin, white bread like air, a casserole crammed with noodles but no meat. He wanted homemade cabbage soup with dense, dark bread, potato pudding with sour cream. He wanted food that took time, love and skill. He wanted food from home. He did not care for insubstantial Canadian fare.

"I no like."

"Oh, you no like," she said, her tone sarcastic.

He did not like her mocking him. He lit a cigarette, inhaled, exhaled. He took his time. Tapping his cigarette on the ashtray's edge, he waited a little longer.

"No like you so much anymore."

Her complexion mottled like red clouds of blood released into water.

"Well, you can just go to hell! You can get the hell out of my house, too, if you don't like what's on offer."

It would be on offer to someone else soon, he thought.

"OK. I stay. If Dobilas and Maryte stay."

"You've got very high opinion of yourself. You think you can just come here and do what you want."

Maybe yes, maybe no. In Lithuania he'd been studying to be a forester. Here he worked in a rubber factory making red white and blue striped balls for children. He would not be a factory worker forever. A better life lay just ahead. And women were much the same everywhere.

"You people," she said. "You stick together."

Yes we do, Steponas thought. We stick together. And for good reason.

"I know what's happened. Maryte's become your floozy."

Steponas leapt up from his chair, sending it scraping backwards.

"You be careful."

"You don't scare me," she said, glaring up at him. "You're all the same. Dirty foreigners."

He almost hit her, this Canadian woman who understood nothing. No soldiers with bayonets would ever enter her kitchen, giving her twenty minutes to prepare for a journey to Siberia. She would never have to beg permission to take a quilt. She would never be pushed roughly out. Living in a country that would never be invaded, she would never be forced to leave.

"You have everything," he said, meaning not just the house but freedom, prosperity and safety. "Why so mean?"

"Not everything," she said, reaching for his hand.

"Bah!" he said, jerking his hand away.

"Wait. I didn't mean it. I take it back."

Steponas waited.

"I'm sorry. Don't go."

Steponas continued waiting.

"Stay. Please."

Steponas waited a little more.

"Maryte and Dobilas can stay, too."

He grunted, refusing to look at her. Satisfying though her concession was, he would never stay now. Dirty foreigner. He would never forgive or forget. And leaving the landlady's kitchen, he went back upstairs to Maryte.

When he told Maryte the story, she looked as if she might throw her arms around his neck. Stepping out of reach of her desperation, he removed himself from the possibility of embrace. He did not like having to disengage himself. He did not like to unlatch their arms. He always travelled alone.

"Where will you go?" she said, her heart sinking. Dobilas sat cross-legged on the bed, pulling at the knobbly fringe on the white chenille bedspread. Where could she hide her brother from a once-friendly woman who had just lost her lover?

"California," he said, squinting off into the distance.

California, a faraway magical place. California, the land of palm trees, sunshine and oranges. Amerika, even better than Canada. It beckoned on the horizon, an even better life.

"Why so far?" she said.

Because dreams live in the distance, he wanted to say. Shaking his head, he tried to dislodge this strange thought that had come out of nowhere and didn't seem to be his.

"Fresh adventures,' he said with a slight smile.

Maryte wondered if he meant new women, a new country, or a new life. One day he would have to stop running. He would have to turn around and look back. You will have to face what you have left, she wanted to tell him. To live with it, as we all do.

Suddenly, she wanted to fling her arms around his neck, asking him to take her with him. Cooking and cleaning, she would take care of Dobilas and him. Please don't leave me, she wanted to say. But they couldn't keep running. Nor could Steponas run forever.

She took his hand and wished him well. She asked him to say goodbye before he left. He nodded, knowing that he wouldn't. He couldn't. Nor could he explain why.

He returned to a room in which he only slept, in a house in which he only ate and had sex. Covering the short distance from Maryte's door to his own, he heard ghosts padding behind him. He slipped into his room.. They slipped in behind him. Standing before him, they watched and waited.

His mother, long dead.

His father, probably dead now, too.

And Agate, his old nurse.

She had taken care of him after his mother died, tending him with an old woman's care. Wrinkled and toothless in a headscarf, she'd offered him shimmering spoonfuls of black-red cherries. He'd taken them into his mouth. He'd closed his eyes and swallowed. And leaving his homeland, driving the horse and wagon to the train station, he'd let her come along.

Take me with you, she had said, placing her wizened arms around his neck.

Take the wagon. Go back, he had said, unlatching her hold.

He sat on the edge of his bed, his face in his hands. Crying without crying, he remembered his nurse, his mother and his country. He cried silently to himself. He cried hoping to be forgiven. He cried wishing to return so that ache in his heart would cease but, until then, to forget.

ꚍꙮ

Maryte helped Dobilas dress for church in the early quiet of Sunday morning. Standing before him, doing up the buttons of his green plaid shirt, she pushed them through the tight holes. Now is the time to tell him, she thought as he looked down, watching the working of her fingers. And chucking him under the chin, she moved the fringe of yellow hair out of his eyes.

"You need a trim," she said.

He settled with delight upon the kitchen stool, the tea towel draped over his shoulders, his head bent, his neck offered to her ministrations.

Strong sunshine filled the room with its sticky glory. Silence surrounded them. Steponas and Mrs. Moynahan still slept, he is his bed, she in hers. Their love, if love it had been, was finished. She would have Dobilas forever. He would always be hers, and she his.

"Time to make the beds," she said, waggling him by the nose then kissing it.

She tucked in the sheets of her double bed while he tidied his cot. Every night they listened to the sounds of one another's breathing as they fell asleep. Every morning they awoke to one another's stirring. Are you awake? he would whisper. Mmmm, she would reply in a sleepy murmur. They had never spent a night apart.

"Let's go to the park first," she said.

Eager and open-mouthed, he slipped his hand into hers.

They stepped into the sparkling morning light, blinking like lovers emerging after a tryst. Squeezing between shiny cars parked along only one side of the street, a long line running from Dundas to Queen, they crossed to the park. We could be taken for husband and wife, she thought, glancing at the windows of the quiet Sunday morning houses. And though the world pitied her unmarried state, she had a love that lasted forever.

They walked across the grass lying before them like their meadow at home. Settling upon a bench, they remembered the whispering swish of grasses, the blueness of meadow flowers, the summer sun upon their smiling faces. She spoke of Ponia Pauliene and Ponas Baliunas, the old widow and widower who had looked after him. He remembered his mischievous twirling in the field. And giggling together, they remembered the old couple's joint enjoyment of grumpiness.

She turned to him. She took his hand. She told him that he would be staying at the church. Father Geras and his housekeeper sister would look after him. It would not be forever.

"Dobilas bad," he said, hanging his head.

"No," she said. "You are not bad."

It was the world that was bad, Nazis and Communists causing the convulsion which had cast them across the ocean. Running, they had left behind the villagers who had kept a firm eye on her brother, the good-natured farm girls who had seen most of life and laughed at it. Danger still lurked here. Dobilas still needed protection. Even if it took separation, she would keep him safe.

"Time to go," she said.

He slipped his hand once more into hers. And her heart broke at his trust.

She returned home, passing the long line of cars parked along one side from Dundas to Queen. Entering the room she and her brother shared, she looked around at the silent emptiness. No soup would simmer on the stove. No brother would wait all day long for her return. And lowering herself into the chair on her side of the table, she sat in a room now only hers.

In his room in the rectory, Dobilas stared at the foreign bed. Lowering himself onto the edge, he looked down at his shoes. If he unlaced them, he would have to take them off. If he took them off, he would have to put his feet on the unfamiliar floor. He would have to lie down. He would have to stay. And humming to himself and rocking on the edge of the bed, he waited for Maryte to fetch him home.

JUSTINE

TORONTO

1951

*Justine remembers nothing except what
Uncle Povilas tells her and he tells her little, only
comforting her when she cries out in the night.*

We are safe, he says. It will not happen again.

But it happens again and again in my head, she says.

*She had been lifted under the armpits and legs and
laid down almost with gentleness upon the forest
floor. A large soldier had loomed over her, blocking
out the glinting sunlight. He had unbuckled his belt.
She had turned her head away. And closing her eyes,
she had listened to the rustling leaves.*

*She had stood on a flat rock in a shallow stream,
washing herself, skirt lifted.*

Then they had continued west.

Chapter 1

Justine and Uncle Povilas stood on the front porch of 2429 Dundas Street West, waiting for their knock to be answered. Their previous landlords, unsettled by Justine's night time cries, had asked them to leave. They are your histories not ours, their uneasy faces said. We wish to sleep. And waiting under the porch overhang, Justine and Uncle Povilas hoped for a new home.

The semi-detached house was painted white and cream, the dark green window trim holding the inharmonious colours together like ribbon around a badly wrapped parcel. The roof sagged where it met its neighbour in the middle. A picture window of plate glass faced the street. The sky was hard blue, the day bright.

"Uncle and niece? You don't say," Doris said, a frowsy unkempt woman in a dark green sweater over which she had tied a soiled cotton apron with thin strings. She removed the cigarette from the corner of her mouth. "Well, it's no business of mine. Live and let live, I always say."

Justine and her uncle exchanged amused smiles.

"You're lucky," Doris said, showing them the room with the picture window. "Nice view."

Close to the street and the noise, Justine thought.

"Main floor," Doris said, tapping her cigarette ash into her palm. "Lucky again."

Footsteps overhead, Justine thought. Evenings. Saturdays. Sundays.

"And it's the biggest room in the house," Doris said.

"Ve take," Povilas said. The city was packed with DPs. Not everyone would take them. They were lucky to find a room at all.

"What's your name?" Doris said, looking around for a place to stub out her cigarette and setting it down on the edge of the windowsill.

"Povilas."

"What's that mean?"

"Paul. But I am Povilas."

"Can't get my tongue round that," she laughed, revealing dull grey teeth. "I'll just call you Paul."

And I'll respond to Povilas.

"And your lady-friend niece?"

"Yes, my niece. Justine."

Perhaps we should call ourselves husband and wife, Justine said to her uncle in Lithuanian.

"Welcome to my house, such as it is," Doris said with a wide sweep of her arm, her rough laugh giving way to a smoker's cough and a fierce pounding on the chest.

Justine stood in the unoccupied room, surrounded by sunshine. Staring down at the bare wooden boards, she saw the forest floor. Bodies lay hidden amid leaves on the ground. If she stirred they would sit up. Holding still, she avoided the soft memory and the dark.

⌒❦⌒

Doris and her husband Jimmy lived on the main floor at the back. Occupying the kitchen and back bedroom, they rented out every other room in the house. One day we're going to up and sell this dump, Doris would laugh. Move to a better locale. And Jimmy, a small man with greasy hair and darting eyes, would laugh along.

Jimmy was a mechanic at the TTC, working nights and sleeping during the day. Rising at 4 p.m., he would wander around the house in his bathrobe, the cord loosely tied at the waist. He would saunter out to the front porch. He would sit and smoke. And relaxing on his veranda, he would view the world of late afternoon.

"How's it going Jimmy-boy?" his neighbours would call out in passing. "How's tricks?"

"None too bad," he would call back, his arm lifted in a lazy wave.

Doris was a haphazard housekeeper, cigarette dangling from her lip as she cleaned. Paying no attention to her husband's sleeping habits, she banged the cupboard doors and wielded the carpet sweeper. She dislodged dirt with rags not themselves clean. Dust shifted to settle elsewhere. The air was grimy with the smell of cooking oil and cigarette smoke.

One day, Justine came up the front steps to find Jimmy sitting on the front porch. Nodding to her landlord, she passed quickly inside. He got up and sauntered in after her.

"Hello, honey," he said placing a hand on her arm. "Feeling friendly?"

She stared down at his hand. Far away from soldiers and war and still not safe.

"C'mon, honey," he said stroking her arm. "A man just can't help hisself, you know? Besides, women like you, well, you kinda like it, don't-cha."

She glared at him. His grey-brown face had as many folds as a bulldog's.

"I tell vife."

"Okay, okay," he said backing off, hands lifted. "Didn't mean nothing by it. You're probably frigid anyway. I bet your *uncle* has no fun with you."

Justine raised her hand, ready to slap him smartly across the face. She held back. She did not wish to touch his flabby grey flesh. She did not wish to touch filth. Tucking her hands into her armpits, she walked away.

❦

Justine's mother had stayed in Lithuania, a widow made harsh by a life with a rough first husband. Her second husband, already old at the time of his marriage, obligingly died not long after from disregard. He had given her another daughter, Elenyte. Audrone made no secret of her preference for her second child. Drawing Povilas and Elenyte close, she tried making a family of three.

Povilas had enough love for all three women in his life. Tossing little Elenyte in the air, he would make her shriek with joy. He would tease Audrone out of her bad moods. He protected Justine from a mother who treated her with daily harshness. Dancing around the three women with good humour, he made life together possible.

"Justine's an artist," he said, watching her head tilt as if she were listening to internal music. "We must send her to Vilnius to study music."

"Go ahead," Audrone said. "I've got everyone I need."

In Vilnius, Justine lived with an aunt and studied at the

conservatory. Spending long sunlit hours in a golden studio filled with music, she flourished. There was an exchange of letters with a famous piano teacher. If you should find yourself in Paris, Madame Boulanger had written, come play for me. And carrying the note in her purse, one handwritten line on a piece of ruled yellow paper, Justine dreamt of a performance career.

One day, Uncle Povilas came to fetch her, saying they must leave. Head filled with the brilliance of music, she had paid scant attention to the boom of Russians guns in the distance. Her uncle insisted. She refused. Finally snatching up her music in frustration, she had let herself be dragged home.

"Audrone we must leave," Povilas said. "All of us. We must go."

"No," she said, eyes flashing as she snatched up little Elenyte. "And you'd better not go either. You'd better stay with me and the child."

Povilas loved all three women equally but loved life and freedom more.

"Then Justine and I will go alone."

They packed one suitcase between them, not wishing to be encumbered. Tucking in her socks next to her uncle's, she thought of the wider world beyond Vilnius, the concert stages of Paris, London and Rome. Rapturous audiences would applaud. Bouquets would land at her feet. And smiling up into up into crowds crying *Bravo!*, she would take her bows.

I carry inside me everything that I need, Justine thought. Liszt had said: Think ten times play once. And closing her eyes, she followed music like thought.

They said farewell in front of the house. Audrone clutched Elenyte to her chest. She glared at them, eyes filled with fury. Then she turned and went into the house.

My mother won't miss me, Justine thought. And little Elenyte will soon forget.

She touched her uncle's arm. He picked up the suitcase. They shared a faint sad smile. Then they turned to face forward. Neither one of them looked back.

They joined the river of refugees moving along the main road. Plodding amid carts piled high with pots and pans, mattresses strapped on top, they were strafed by aircraft. They leapt sideways into a ditch. They lifted their heads to see neighbours lying dead, their limbs askew. And leaving the main road to travel cross-country, they met the soldiers in the woods.

When the war was over, Justine and Povilas stood on the pier at Bremerhaven amid crowds of DPs boarding a ship for Canada. They clustered together like children, large cardboard tags hanging from the buttons of their coats. The men were assigned to mining or forestry work, the women to hospital or domestic service. After ten months, they would be free to do what they liked. Bereft, hungry and lost, they were eager for safety and work and plenty to eat.

Justine became a domestic in the home of the Morgensterns, a rich family of German Jewish extraction. Completing her contract, she was offered a permanent position. She agreed to stay. She was happy to have a job. And in a city crammed with DPs telling stories of harsh treatment, she had fair employers.

When Father Geras asked her to play the organ at Sunday mass, she shook her head. Bach and Handel had sat in similar seats, sending their music resounding into the church. Father Geras offered her the use of the organ anyway. He suggested a little concert. Waving him away in panic, she said she couldn't.

She could not explain the feelings jostling inside her. Pressing their faces forward, they insisted upon being seen. Loneliness for her life in Vilnius. Anger and bitterness at her loss. Discontent at the company of farmers rather than musicians. Guilt and happiness at being safe. Hearing only silence where music had once lived, she dreaded that this might be her life forever, silent, empty and flat.

Povilas finished his contract at the lumber camp in the north woods, joining her in Toronto. Finding a job at Neilsen's Chocolate Factory, standing all day long by a large copper cauldron, he stirred melted chocolate. Did you go to the church to practice? he would ask coming home from his shift. Did you play? And she would turn her head away, silent and bitter.

It's dead and gone, she thought. And I can't bring it back.

Chapter 2

Harry Morgenstern was a lawyer, a tall elegant man, sophisticated and well-dressed. Comfortable in his clothes, he never felt the need to adjust his shirt cuffs or to cross and uncross his long legs. He was at ease with himself and his place in the world. He loved his wife Greta. And still loving her after thirty years, he felt no desire for dalliance.

At the end of the war, he had gone with The United Nations Relief and Rehabilitation Administration to help sort out the mess in Europe. Returning after six months amid blackened cities and rubble, he told Greta that he wished to take on a refugee maid. Greta had put up with his long absences. She had borne them without complaint. While he was overseeing the fates of strangers, she and the children had fended for themselves.

"Haven't you done enough, Harry? Is it also necessary to bring one of them into our home?"

"But surely that is just what *is* needed."

Harry had come upon Greta driving a cab in early 1930s Berlin. Tidying up legal affairs for his far-sighted father who had moved the family from unfriendly Germany to New York, he had fallen in love with this sparky young girl who took no guff from strangers. His family protested the marriage. They referred to her forever after as "that wretched girl that Harry had plucked from the gutter." Neither forgiving nor forgetting, Greta attended to her husband's every happiness.

"With such good fortune as ours," Mr. Morgenstern said, "we would be remiss not to help."

Mrs. Morgenstern found herself outmanoeuvred and silenced in one lawyerly stroke.

The Morgensterns lived in a grand house with a large black-and-white foyer, its tall oak doors opening onto spacious rooms filled with French antiques, Persian carpets and Italian chandeliers. On business trips Harry would stay in the New York apartment he had inherited from his father. In May and September Mrs. Morgenstern would visit Sak's Fifth Avenue. At Christmas they would go to see the glittering lights of the Rockefeller Center. On weekends, they might visit Carnegie Hall and the Guggenheim Museum.

"The apartment's small, really just big enough for family," Mrs. Morgenstern would tell friends never invited along.

Mr. Morgenstern confined himself to legal matters, leaving domestic affairs to his wife. Venturing an opinion now and then on schools or cooks, he would encounter a swift response. You may know business Harry, she would say, but I know people. He stayed out of her sphere. To this and the steady influx of money he attributed the success of his thirty year marriage.

They were incredibly wealthy. They sent their four sons to the finest schools and, upon graduation, on European tours. They dined out in the best restaurants four times a week. They threw dinner parties, lavish affairs with flowers and champagne, sumptuous feasts. They had the ease of the equally matched and long married. And moving under the soft light of chandeliers and among guests upon whom life had not bestowed equal good fortune, they were envied their beautiful and bountiful life.

❦

Justine cleaned the living room, a spacious room filled with antiques and art. Wiping small ormolu-encrusted tables and heavy gilt picture frames, she avoided the piano, a white baby grand with a glossy sheen. She never touched it. She never looked at it. Dusting furniture set far enough apart for easy mingling, she sensed the piano's pearly white presence, a ghost hovering at the back of her mind.

At parties, Mr. Morgenstern would play for admiring friends. Mrs. Morgenstern would lean on the lid, enraptured and misty-eyed, martini in hand. I play better than that, Justine would think, moving among the guests in the black and white maid's outfit required for parties. And listening with a faint smile, she would offer canapés on a silver tray.

Mrs. Morgenstern collected Royal Doulton figurines, displaying "her pretty ladies" on the mantelpiece. Receiving a new one every Christmas from an indulgent husband, she would fall upon her present with delight. What a lucky girl I am! she would cry. And bestowing a kiss upon her husband's silvery head, she would place the newcomer on the mantle.

January sunshine filled the room with winter warmth. Washing the figurines in warm soapy water, Justine admired the voluminous skirts filled with motion, the china perfection of arms and necks. Autumn Breeze, one hand to her hat, her green skirts lifted by wind. Marguerite, coquettish in an off-the-shoulder crimson gown. And Fiona, simple and still in a fall of cobalt blue. Wiping them dry, she wondered if a world of such ladies existed, their days glossy and smooth.

Outside the window, an icicle cracked. She went over to the piano. She hit C sharp. She snatched her hand away. The note shimmered pitch perfect in the air.

She sat down, lifted her hands and played. Releasing the strength in her shoulders and arms, she landed resounding chords. She raced up and down scales. She rilled along arpeggios and trills. In the quiet sunlit room, music came rushing back, filling her with relief and delight.

"You're a pianist," Mr. Morgenstern said from the doorway.

She leapt up from the bench.

"I study in my country," she said.

"Do you play now?"

How could I? she wanted to snap at this well-mannered gentleman. His politeness stifled any silly retorts.

"No piano," she said.

"Use mine," he said. "Please. A talent like yours should not be allowed to languish."

Justine did not understand *languish* but understood the offer. Fear vied with wild hope in her breast.

"But Mrs. Morgenstern ...," she said.

"Oh you leave Greta to me," he said with the pleased puckishness of a man who didn't mind the mild sport of riling his wife. "Would you play for me now? Please? It would give me the greatest pleasure."

She played, racing up and down the stairs of Scarlatti and Bach, swooping upon the currents of Chopin, rippling along the rivers of Ravel.

"What's going on here?" Mrs. Morgenstern said, setting

down bags from Creeds and taking in her husband leaning back in his favourite wing chair with cognac and cigar in hand and her maid's behind on the piano bench.

"Why just as you see, my dear," Mr. Morgenstern said with the mild patience of an unexcitable man. "Justine is playing the piano. Did you know she was such a talent?"

Mrs. Morgenstern turned to Justine. "Take these bags up to my room."

Justine leapt up, hurrying forward to relieve Mrs. Morgenstern of her expensive shopping. Carrying the bags to the master bedroom, she could hear husband and wife arguing. Her talent is for worming her way into other people's lives, Mrs. Morgenstern shouted. What will you have her doing next? Playing for our guests? Justine placed the bags on the closet floor and hurried back downstairs.

"I no play," she said from the doorway.

"How many times have I told you not to enter a room when people are talking?" Mrs. Morgenstern said. "I will not have my maids eavesdropping. Even someone like you should be able to understand that."

"Greta, there's no need for that," Mr. Morgenstern said.

Mrs. Morgenstern glared at her husband then turned and left the room.

Mr. Morgenstern sighed.

"Justine, your first duties are as housemaid. You must do as my wife says and do it well. But the piano needs playing. It doesn't get played enough by me. Practice in your spare time if you wish. As to my wife," he said, raising a hand to still her objection, "I will take care of it."

He left the room, pursuing his wife and peace.

Trouble trouble trouble, Justine thought, resuming her

cleaning, her strokes keeping rhythm with her thoughts. No good to make trouble between husband and wife. No good for job. No good for me.

The next morning, Justine found herself heaped with work. Moving the furniture away from walls, climbing upon chairs, she cleaned in behind cupboards and along the tops of lintels. For the first time, she heard complaints about her work. You cannot break me, she thought. I have had tougher masters than you. Polishing the silverware stretching along the glossy dining room table like a shiny landscape, she worked in a fury.

Mrs. Morgenstern left for the afternoon, pulling on long dove grey gloves with satisfaction. Putting down her cloth, Justine went over to the piano. She lifted the lid, sat down and played, once more in the golden studio in Vilnius. She played in the sunlight of memory. Then rising and closing the lid, she made sure the lady of the house found her dusting the piano when she came home.

⟡

Justine stood at the stove, cooking breakfast for the Morgensterns. Shifting the eggs in the pan, she watched her employers reading the *Globe and Mail* at the kitchen table. The wife liked scrambled, the husband sunny side up. Mr. Morgenstern always insisted that Greta be served first. And lifting his cup for coffee, he said that Tony Ursell, a colleague on the board at the Royal Conservatory of Music, had agreed to hear Justine play.

Mrs. Morgenstern kept her face turned carefully to the paper.

"Thank you, Mr. Morgenstern," Justine said. "Thank you but I no ready."

"Nonsense," Mr. Morgenstern said. "You were ready the moment I heard you. And now that you've been practising you'll be even better. Shall we say next Saturday? I'm sure Greta can manage breakfast on her own that day."

"Of course, I can. Of course, she must go," Mrs. Morgenstern said, glancing up. "Our budding pianist."

Justine hesitated. Refusing would offend Mr. Morgenstern, accepting would displease Mrs. Morgenstern. She might lose her job. But if I could play it wouldn't matter, she thought. I could leave this work behind. And heart leaping, she resolve to take this chance to regain her musical life.

"Thank you," Justine said. "Thank you."

"It's settled then." Mr. Morgenstern sat back, beaming.

Mrs. Morgenstern stared at her, eyes glittering.

Justine set breakfast before her employers. Mr. addressed his sunny-side-up eggs with delight. Mrs. Morgenstern, licking her finger and lightly flicking a page, let her scrambled eggs get cold beside her. A morning silence descended. And Justine felt herself dismissed.

Chapter 3

Justine did not wish to marry. Responding to Uncle Povilas' teasing that a woman's route to happiness lay through a man, she would cry out in mock horror. A man? I'd have to spend all day cooking and cleaning. How could I be a pianist when I'd have to mend a husband's socks? And bantering back, she would coast upon mischief.

Povilas persisted, raising the subject from time to time. He had taken her away from Lithuania. He had been unable to protect her in the woods. She had been a pianist. Now she was a housemaid. His sense of responsibility and guilt were boundless.

"A young man might be just what you need," he would tease in his usual manner.

"I don't wish it," Justine said.

"But you can't live alone forever. It's too hard for a woman. Look at your mother."

"What has my mother got to do with it? And I am not alone. I have music."

"It is not enough. Not in this world. Not in this life."

How can you decide what is enough for me? Justine thought, holding back harsh words.

"It is what I want," she said to the protective uncle who had encouraged her talent, sent her to study in Vilnius and brought her to safety here.

"You must have a home and a family. You must have something to do."

"I have a family. You. And I wish to play music, not house."

Oh my dear, can you not see that no career will happen for you here? Povilas thought. You are seen only as a housemaid. They will not give you a chance, not over their own pianists. Why would they prefer an outsider to one of their own?

When she brought home the news about the audition, he remained silent.

"What's the matter Uncle Povilai? You don't seem very happy for me."

"I am happy. Very happy."

"No, you're not. You're not happy at all. You surprise me."

Oh my dear, Povilas thought, can you not see they are just being kind to you? Nothing will come of it.

"I don't want you to be disappointed. Or hurt."

Once again I will not be able to protect you, he thought.

"Have faith, Uncle. Music has returned."

"I have faith. In *you*. But these Canadians. They see us differently from how we see ourselves."

And they put their own people first, he thought. As do we.

"Don't worry," Justine said. "When they hear me play they will see what I can do. And everything will change. Oh, I'm so happy."

Who knows, Povilas thought as Justine planted a kiss upon his forehead. Perhaps these Canadians will see the gem in their midst. If not, it will be better if she realizes it herself.

Justine burrowed into him just as she had as a child when he came home on leave from the army. Returning resplendent in his uniform with gold braid and brass buttons, he had left her and her mother gaping in adoration. He had placed an arm around each. He had drawn them close. And leaving off kneading her bitterness into the dough, her mother had allowed herself to be embraced.

The following Saturday Povilas rang the doorbell of the Morgensterns' grand house. Rocking back and forth on his heels, glancing down at his well-polished shoes, he waited for Mrs. Morgenstern to answer the door. He had not told Justine he was going. She would have flung herself at him, crying not to interfere. But like a father determined to sniff out the intentions of a daughter's suitor he had come to assess Justine's chances.

"Yes?" Mrs. Morgenstern said, looking him up and down, cold and quick.

"I am Povilas. Uncle of Justine," he said, removing his hat. Was this the warm friendly woman Justine had described?

"What do you want?"

"To talk." Was the woman going to make him speak from the doorstep like a salesman, hat in hand? Was she not going to ask him to step inside? What manners these Canadians had.

"How do I know you are who you say you are?" she said, eyes narrowing.

"I come about Justine," he said reaching for patience. Really this woman was ridiculous. And stupid.

"Ah," Mrs Morgenstern said. "In that case, come in."

He stepped into the spacious black and white tiled foyer, a room requiring six or seven strides to cross. It was large enough to dance in though Mrs. Morgenstern didn't strike him as the dancing type. She didn't seem like the woman Justine had described. Had his niece not been telling him the whole truth? And holding the hat which Mrs. Morgenstern had not offered to take from him, he looked around.

"Is husband home?"

"I run the household. If you have something to say, say it to me. If the girl wants to quit, she should have come so herself. Not sent her uncle."

"I come about music."

"Ah. Music. Well, what can I say? My husband has arranged an audition. The rest is up to her. Though after all we've done for her, it's really beyond the pale to send her uncle on her behalf." She turned away and lit a cigarette.

"I only ask opinion. What chance for my Justine?"

"What chance? Well I'd say that depends entirely on her. My husband says she can play but—how shall I put it, " she drew on her cigarette, "she'll need more than that. For example, how's her English? She'll be before the public. She'll need ... oh I don't know"—she made a graceful gesture in the air with her cigarette—"a certain je ne sais quoi" She inhaled again then settled a look upon him. "Do you think that your niece can do all that?"

Povilas's heart sank with every word.

"Mr. Morgenstern, what he say?" Povilas said.

"My husband is entitled to his opinion."

Entitled? What did entitled mean?

"I speak with husband."

Mrs. Morgenstern jabbed her cigarette into a chrome pedestal ashtray.

"Sure. Let me get him for you."

"So you are the uncle," Mr. Morgenstern said, approaching with a smile and a hand outstretched. "Your niece is very talented. But you already know that. And you know about the audition. I trust that's why you're here? We will do our absolute best to help her. Just make her practice. She needs to build up her confidence."

Povilas looked from husband to wife and back to husband again. How could such a nice man be married to such an awful woman? Perhaps he was more interested in Justine than in her music. It wouldn't be surprising. It wouldn't be the first time. Suspicion leapt like a crouched cat, sudden and silent.

"Why you do this?"

"Because she has talent. I hate to see it languish."

Languish? What did languish mean?

"What did you *think* I had in mind? Look, my good fellow, if you're thinking what I think you're thinking, you've got it all wrong."

Povilas became lost in the twists and turns of this sentence.

"If you want me to back off I certainly will though I think it would be a shame," Mr. Morgenstern continued. "And what about Justine herself? What does she want?"

By now Povilas had caught up with Mr. Morgenstern's meaning. He began to feel alarmed. He should not have come. He should not have interfered. He had made things worse.

"Please," he said, striving to find words which became even more elusive when he was upset.

"Please you want me to stop? Or please you want me to continue?"

Povilas worked the brim of his hat round and round in anguish.

"What did I tell you, Harry?" Mrs. Morgenstern said. "These people don't know how to behave. They control their women. They tell them what to do. It doesn't matter what they want. I know you can't bear to be unkind but it's better to be too hard than too soft. To not get taken advantage of. Can you see that now?"

"Be quiet, Greta," Mr. Morgenstern said.

Mrs. Morgenstern shrugged and lit another cigarette.

"Listen my good man," Mr. Morgenstern said. "I have no designs on your niece. But talent like hers should be brought to the world. And I want to do it." He smiled. "When she is famous I will be able to look back and say, I had a small hand in that."

Povilas sensed the man's sincere intention. He seized his hand, pumping it up and down.

"You good man. You very good man."

"I'm just happy to help," Mr. Morgenstern said, patting him awkwardly on the shoulder.

Povilas shook Mr. Morgenstern's hand once again. Mrs. Morgenstern watched, cigarette in hand. He inclined his head in her direction. He was not worried. The husband would prevail.

Outside, Povilas paused on the front steps, putting on his fedora. Tipping his head back, he looked up at the fresh blue sky. Who knows, he thought. Maybe things would turn out alright. And descending the concentric half-circles of flagstone, he re-entered the street leading away from the Morgensterns' world.

❦

At home, he tried not to tell her. In the end, he could not keep it from her. She threw her arms around him in joy. Her face shone with happiness. Suddenly she withdrew.

"They will think that I asked you to go," she said. She could not say that her uncle had gone of his own accord. Nor would they believe it. She would be judged on circumstance. She would have to live under the misunderstanding. She would have to let it stand.

Povilas went silent. The thought had never occurred to him.

"Don't worry. Her husband convinced her." In any event the woman would do what her husband said. And when Justine was embarked on a piano career it wouldn't matter.

"Oh uncle, might I really have a chance?" Justine said, her face flooding with hope. "Do you really think that maybe ..."

"Let us hope so," he said, praying all the while that God who had once been so cruel would now be kind.

They made dinner in a room with no running water and no stove. Standing side by side, they cooked on a green two-burner hotplate. Justine fried patties in a small skillet. Povilas spooned potatoes out of boiling water. And sitting down to eat, a breathless peace and happiness prevailed.

❦

The next morning, Justine put her pink sweater over her nightgown and went into the Doris's kitchen. Carrying a bucket, she emptied yesterday's dishwater down the drain. She turned on the tap. Water pummelled into the pail. And dreaming along to the drumming rhythm, she waited for the bucket to fill.

Jimmy drifted out of the bedroom yawning and stretching. Mouth falling open to reveal an unattractive cavern, his eyes came to rest on her. He smacked his mouth shut. He looked at her bare legs. And bathrobe spreading open at the knees, he lowered himself into a kitchen chair.

"I could get you some stockings. Would you like that? Would you, huh?"

Stockings? Who did he think he was? An American GI?

"I was over there myself. Saw action. Even got wounded. Still a bit of shrapnel here," he said, rubbing his thigh. "Everything else is in good working order, if you know what I mean. So what about those stockings? Want some?"

"No. Thank you." Justine was surprised that he had helped to liberate but war brought out courage and cowardice in the most unexpected places. All the same it didn't give him rights.

"The way I see it," he said leaning forward, "you kinda owe me. For saving you from those nasty Nazis."

Justine recoiled.

"All us boys fighting over there. And for who? You. Lots of 'em died. You should think about that. Show us poor boys a little appreciation."

"You sick." You disgust me, she wanted to say but didn't have the English words.

"Sick? No way! I'm healthy as a horse. Here. I'll show ya," he said, rising and starting to open to his bathrobe.

Justine ran out of the kitchen and smack into Doris. The woman stood before her, placid and stout in her nightdress, her round stomach protruding.

"Has Jimmy been bothering you, honey? Pay him no mind. He can't do anything. There's nothing there if you know what I mean. Poor boy," she said, her eyes flicking over her husband with a softness that Justine had never seen. "Go to bed now, Jimmy. You need your rest."

Jimmy pushed himself up from the table with sudden weariness. He shuffled back to the bedroom. He shut the door.

"Take no notice, honey," Doris said turning to Justine. "He can't hurt you. He couldn't hurt a fly." She gazed after him. "The equipment doesn't work anymore. This is the only type fun he can have. Poor lad," she added, shaking her head with a soft chuckle.

Justine had not expected this. She had not expected bravery in Jimmy and understanding in Doris. She had not expected such tenderness between husband and wife. She was envious of a world in which such things happened.

Doris rested her eyes upon Justine. "Jimmy's told me many things about what happened over there. It can't have been easy for you, dear. Tell me what happened. Tell me what's eating you. Get rid of it honey. Unburden yourself. It'll make you feel a whole lot better."

Justine had not expected this either, sympathy from a woman on this side of the Atlantic. Standing in her nightgown in the kitchen, she turned towards this woman to whom she had paid scant attention. For a moment she wanted to fall into her sturdy embrace. She could not. And leaving with a grateful nod, she retreated to her side of experience.

Chapter 4

The morning of the audition dawned moist and tender, the sky a soft blue. Walking to the streetcar, passing houses resting side by side, their verandas offering shelter, Justine felt the peacefulness. No bombs fell here. Nothing catastrophic occurred, nothing but daily life. Moving through the morning freshness of the quiet treed street, she felt a rising hope.

She would be playing for strangers. She was familiar with the strangers of her country but these would be English strangers. They listened with different ears. They thought different thoughts. When she played, would they hear a pianist or a DP suitable only for cleaning houses?

"Trust your talent," Uncle Povilas had said. "Remember what you were back home. A pianist. A good pianist. Remember who you still are."

She had kissed the top of his head, an uncle beaten unconscious by the forest soldiers and unable to protect her but blaming himself still.

She was taking the Dundas streetcar, changing at the cleft at College. Watching it approach from the distance, she remembered the train pulling into the station in Berlin.

Uncle Povilas had clambered aboard. In a starfish spread, he had claimed seats. Travelling westward, moving ever further away from family and home, she had gazed out the window.

Would her mother be sitting by the window, missing her? Were she to come running back, would she accept her? Would she take her into her embrace? She did not think so. Her mother would be stroking Elenyte's golden hair, whispering and holding her close.

With a twitch of irritation she sent the memories away. Waiting in the gentle morning light, she imagined a concert hall filled with applause, a conductor bowing to kiss her hand. She would place a hand to her breast. She would give a deep graceful curtsey. And picking up the lavish bouquets thrown at her feet, she would refuse the tuxedoed young men waiting backstage to take her to dinner.

The cream and red streetcar arrived, coasting to a stop. It settled with a heavy whoosh. The doors opened with rattling jerks.

I wish to live in music, she though. Nothing more.

She stepped up, clasping the cool steel pole. Dropping her ticket into the glass and metal box, she watched it land soft and limp on the black velvety bottom. The jaws of a trap door snapped open and shut. Her ticket dropped out of sight. Losing her balance as the streetcar jerked forward, she reached again for the slippery steel pole.

"Steady there, miss," the conductor said, placing a hand at the small of her back.

Justine stiffened at his touch. She twisted to look down at him. His face held only concern. She eased. People here could be so kind.

She sat down beside a woman looking out the window,

a middle-aged woman in a brown coat and kerchief. Clutching an old black leather bag in her lap, she stared into the street with the fixed rigidity of sadness. What unhappiness lies in this woman's heart? Justine thought. Is she thinking of someone? And her thoughts tumbled backwards to the ship crossing the Atlantic.

She had been alone on deck, walking in the early morning mist. A young woman stood with both hands on the rails, staring with determination into the sea. She's going to jump, Justine thought, starting forward with alarm. Pulled round by her presence, the girl stopped her with a commanding look.

Do not interfere, her face said. My life is mine to do with as I wish.

She launched herself ever so lightly in a graceful arc over the rails. For a split second, she hovered suspended in the air. She seemed to float. Then she plunged with a soundless splash into the sea.

Justine rushed to the rails with a cry. Leaning over, she searched the waters for a wet bobbing head. No arm waved. No plea for help came. She saw only the empty heaving of a dark sea.

So many people had died, Justine thought, staring out the streetcar window. So many.

The streetcar stopped. The Conservatory came into view. She had arrived.

～❧～

Tony Ursell was a tall gingerish man edging towards middle age. Rising from behind the table, coming towards her with outstretched hand, he had the self-deprecating charm of a man who considered himself attractive to women. He's probably very successful, she thought. Often. And taking his hand, she felt his senses quicken like a hound scenting prey.

"So you're a musician," he said. "A real pianist, Morgenstern says. Let's see what you can do." And he gestured towards the piano bench.

She played Scarlatti, her hands sparkling upon the keys. Moving around her, he paced with the music. She felt the keenness of his pleasure. It was a surrounding kindness. Lifting her hands off the keyboard with relaxed grace, she waited for his response.

"That was sublime. Almost religious."

His hand landed on the nape of her neck. She jumped up and drew back.

"No," she said. "Please. I no like."

"But I do," Ursell said, approaching with a knowing look.

"No," she said, her tone sharp.

Ursell stopped. "What shall we do here then?"

Justine felt tears spring to her eyes. The price of music was bed.

She turned her head away, considering whether to sleep with him. Imagining his freckled hands upon her flesh, she knew his touch would not be tender. His cool blue eyes held a look of imminent victory. Her stomach lurched. She could not do it, not even for music.

He cupped her chin with his hand. She proudly lifted her face away.

"Have it your way then," he said, releasing her with the relaxed unconcern of a man who knew that, if not her, then someone else.

Tai viskas, she thought. That was it. There would be no other chances.

He sauntered back to his table, settling back into his seat. Politeness dictated that she should thank him, shake his hand and say goodbye. She rebelled against the forced nature of the transaction. She could not bear the prospect of touch. Deciding that lack of nicety could make no difference now, she left.

⌘

The next morning, Justine found Mrs. Morgenstern sitting in the living room. Wearing pearls, a grey silk dress and pale sling-back pumps, she was smoking and reading a magazine. She flicked a page. She did not look up. And going over to the mantle, Justine started cleaning the pretty ladies.

"You're back," Mrs. Morgenstern said, still not looking up.

"Yes, Mrs." *What did she think? I still have to work.*

"Well, we'll see about that."

Mrs. Morgenstern rose, stubbed out her cigarette and came over to the mantle. Picking up Autumn Breeze between thumb and forefinger, she held her by her thin china neck. She opened her fingers. She let her drop. And the young woman in the billowing ochre coat, one small china hand held to her green hat smashed into skittering pieces on the floor.

"Mrs. Morgenstern," Justine gasped, "what you do?"

"Too bad you're so clumsy. One of my favourites. Such an expensive piece, too. Mr. Morgenstern is not going to be happy when he finds out."

Justine remained silent. It would be no use to speak. As Mr. himself had said, Mrs. was in charge of the house. It was not fair but fair did not apply to DP maids. And seeing the twitch of Mrs. Morgenstern's small smile, Justine knew the moment to have been planned.

"I see we understand one another," Mrs. Morgenstern said.

You understand nothing, Justine thought. Nothing nothing nothing.

Suddenly the invisible soldiers on the forest floor sat up. They smacked their palms on the ground. They opened their mouths and roared. Stop, Justine cried inside her head. Oh please stop. And with the hefty sweep of both arms, she sent the figurines smashing to the floor.

Mrs. Morgenstern stared at the china arms and heads scattered on the floor. Stooping to collect the broken pieces, she gazed up stricken. What have you got to be upset about? Justine snorted. It's just china, not real people. Regaining her composure the lady of the house slowly rose.

"You are discharged. And good riddance to bad rubbish."

"Rubbish," Justine said. "Hah. You are rubbish."

Mrs. Morgenstern's face went red. She pointed to the door.

"Leave my house."

"Oh, yes," Justine said. "I go. With pleasure."

Head held high, she marched towards the door. She yanked it open. She stepped through it and slammed it shut. And standing in the quiet street, blinking in the sunshine, she began to shake.

Chapter 5

In the fall, Justine fell ill. She took to her bed, lying all day long on her side beneath a sheet. She clamped her lips shut like a stubborn child. She refused the food Uncle Povilas offered on an outstretched spoon. Turning her head away, lying inert with her back to the world, she had become the woman in the streetcar, pinned by sadness.

Povilas called Dr. Prizura. Everyone knew the story of the good doctor who had saved the child choking on a plum stone in High Park. He had a practice on Bloor Street. He had a wife and child. He was the pride of the community though it was rumoured that the marriage wasn't happy.

Dr. Prizura looked down at the body beneath the sheet, the contours like the low mounds of an ancient mountain range covered in snow. Her body was not sick. It was her soul. An illness of the spirit. He saw it often enough.

"We must get her up," he said. "We must get her out of bed."

The two men hauled her up, acting as one. Taking hold of an arm each, slinging it over their shoulders, they made her walk. She was like a suicide whose stomach had been pumped of pills. She must be kept awake. They marched back and forth, Justine hanging between them, her feet dragging.

"Walk," the doctor commanded. "Walk."

He slapped her smartly across the face. Once. Twice.

She moaned but her legs began to move.

When the danger had passed he lay her back down on the bed. Bathing her back as she lay on her stomach, running the sponge along her naked curve, his mind slid back to the moment under the linden trees when he had learned of Lidia's death. You no longer have the right to die, he thought looking down at this woman breathing with her face in the pillow. You belong to all of us now, not just to yourself.

"You must go on living. For those who didn't."

The words landed upon Justine like a soft rain. She saw a sunlit studio with gleaming wood floors. She saw a silent piano. She gave a deep shudder. The vision slid away. And closing her eyes, she slept.

⌒❦⌒

She got a job at Canada Packers, working the restaurant line. Scooping up handfuls of bacon sliced by a whirling blade, she slung them into long cardboard boxes lined with wax paper. She worked 3:25 p.m.–11:55 p.m., for the shift premium. Nights paid even more. Uneasy at the long stretch of stillness and dark, she stuck to what was called "afternoons".

She would go to the women's locker room, changing street clothes for a white coat and a hairnet. Wrapping the cotton robe around her, criss-crossing it over her breasts, she would cinch the waist tight. She tucked every strand of her hair under the net. She rubbed her lips clean of lipstick. And bracing herself for the long walk to her station, she joined the other women.

They travelled in a tight clutch through the noisy cavernous factory, running the gauntlet of working men. Hooting and hollering, whistling and stamping their feet, the waiting males called out invitations. The women huddled together. They hurried past at just below a run. And trying not to get stuck on the outside, Justine sought the refuge of the middle.

Justine worked, listening to the women chattering around her. Having sent husbands to work and children to school, having cleaned house and cooked the day's meals, they put in a shift for extra money. She liked the easy talk of domestic difficulties. She liked distraction and laughter. Then came the end of shift and the ride home after midnight.

She would stand on the street with the other women, waiting in the dark for the streetcar. Looking along St. Clair, seeing the lit car approaching, she would will it to hurry. She would urge the doors to open. She asked them to admit her to safety. Riding home, she wished she could remain within the protective light.

She descended into her late-night street. She hurried through the dark. She had to get into the house. She had to shut the door. She had to keep the forest men out. Safe inside, she leaned against the door.

Will it always he like this? she thought, chest heaving.

One day she caught sight of Steponas looking at her in Lithuania House. Rumour had it that Mrs. Moynahan had kicked him out. He'd gone to California where he'd tried his hand at many things. Returned, he was welcomed back as one of their own by a community that stuck together.

I have to do something, she thought as he approached, a cocky smile on his lips. It may as well be this.

"You are the famous pianist," he said.

"Was," she said. She liked the sound of famous.

"All of us were something else once upon a time."

She made an appreciative murmur. He caught her note of satisfaction.

"You like the truth then?"

"Yes. Always. Then I know what to do."

"I will always tell you the truth. You can count on me for that."

They started going on picnics in High Park, the three of them, Justine, Steponas and Povilas. Billowing out a blanket, they would settle down on a hilltop overlooking Grenadier Pond and the garden shaped like a maple leaf. Justine would set out pickles, ham, dark dense bread and, sometimes, strawberries. They would eat. Then leaning back they would lounge, masters of pleasures that cost nothing.

They talked of life back home. Povilas described military life and the camaraderie of the barracks. Steponas spoke of swimming in a lake while hanging onto his horse's tail. We had no choice but to leave, they would say, struggling with the words traitor, deserter, selfish. Conversation kept at bay the remorse and the guilt, the longing for home and the deep wish for return.

They spoke of the present. They discussed the Sunday Lithuanian Radio Hour introduced by a rousing march from *Aida*, the Saturday morning children's school in the church basement, the summer camp at Springhurst Beach in Wasaga. They argued over which was the better newspaper, Toronto's *The Lights of Homeland* or Montreal's *Independent Lithuania*. Buoyed and uplifted, they never forgot that life here was temporary.

The talk would turn to the future. Losing hope that the West would push the Communists out, they wondered how long Stalin could last. They did not speak of those left behind. Memories were too miserable, feelings too hard to admit. Reaching the territory of no further words, they fell quiet at the thought of going home.

Justine remained silent. She did not like to remember her mother's cruelties, her lost career, the forest soldiers. She did not like to think of Mrs. Morgenstern's broken pretty ladies or Tony Ursell's freckled hand on the nape of her neck. She did not think they would all return, joyfully, home. Life can't be made right, she thought. And bitterness pushed the vision aside, occupying the place where love and longing had once lived.

"I only miss one thing," she blurted out, having had enough of nostalgic ramblings and ill-placed hopes. "My little sister Elenyte."

"Perhaps you need a baby of your own," Steponas said.

She knew then that he was serious about her. And next Sunday, leaning on his elbow with a casual air, Steponas suggested that they should marry.

"You would be happy with me," he said.

Yes, of course I would, she thought. If everyone else can be happy, why can't I?

She nodded. Povilas nodded too, with relief, his job done.

⁂

Justine asked Doris to be Maid of Honour. Flattered and flustered, Doris buzzed around the kitchen making the wedding luncheon. She had thrown an apron over a black lace dress with deep scalloped edges. She wore low pumps with square toes and square heels. Sturdy on strong legs, moving between stove and kitchen table, she dished out chicken, potato salad and jiggly green jello.

Where did she get that dress? Justine thought. How did this woman who wore shapeless clothes and a pair of Jimmy's fleece lined slippers, the backs cut out with a kitchen knife, come to have such a dress in her closet?

"Oh, I was quite a catch in my prime," she said, noticing Justine's look. "Quite a prime it was too, if I say so myself. Wasn't it Jimmy?" She raised a coquettish hand to the back of her hair, a French roll spiralling upwards like a tornado.

"It sure was, honey. It sure was. You were gorgeous."

Doris harrumphed at this back-handed compliment then continued.

"We went dancing every Friday night, didn't we, Jimmy? Sometimes on Sundays, too. Cut quite a rug, didn't we Jimmy?"

"We sure did, honey bunch. We sure did."

They smiled at one another, kind indulgent smiles filled with private pleasures and love.

Doris rose. She took Jimmy by the hand. She placed him into her embrace, stout woman leading, skinny man attached like an apron to her front. And moving in a serene and stately fashion to music that only they could hear, they danced in a kitchen become a ballroom.

"Whew that was fun," Doris said, dropping back down into her chair, her French roll unravelling. "We should do that more often. We should go out together. All of us. We're friends, ain't we?" she added with a sweep of her arm.

Everyone nodded. Then Povilas announced that he

would be moving out so that Steponas and Justine could have the room.

"Of course!" Doris cried. "There must be room for the baby."

Nudging one another with knowing winks, rocking an imaginary baby, Doris and Jimmy sang.

> *Rock a bye baby*
> *In the tree top*
> *When the wind blows*
> *The cradle will rock*
> *When the bough breaks*
> *The cradle will fall*
> *And down will come baby*
> *Cradle and all*

Steponas grinned. Povilas slapped him on the back. Jimmy fell into a coughing fit. Doris smacked him on the back. Justine blushed and looked down.

"Pay them no mind, honey," Doris said, words slurring. "They're jes' men. Silly ol' men. But we love 'em, don't we?" And swivelling her face 'round, chin sunk into her palm, she gave Jimmy a happy look.

For a moment Justine caught a glimpse of a world where kindliness and good nature prevailed, where men's wrongdoings were nothing more than minor character flaws laughed off by tolerant women. Forests did not contain the raucous laughter of soldiers and the clink of belt buckles. Misunderstandings did not lead to war. Evil did not flourish. She wished it were true but history, bitterness and a sense of grievance pushed the vision away.

The party drew to a close. Rising unsteadily to her feet, Doris planted a sloppy kiss on Justine's forehead. She gave her a mischievous little shove towards the bedroom.

"Off you go now," she said with a giggle. "You have work to do."

Six months later, Justine was pregnant.

⁓⊕⁓

Steponas wanted to name their daughter Veronika, after his mother. Holding her daughter in her arms, waiting for the flood of happiness to fill her, she nodded her absent agreement. What if I can't love her? she thought, looking down at the sucking mouth, the clenched flailing fists. And feeling nothing but rising panic, she thrust the little creature back at the glowing nurse.

Steponas brought a gift to the hospital, presenting it to his wife as she lay in bed. Letting him place the pretty silver watch on her wrist, she struggled not to pull away. What is wrong with me? she thought, wanting to be grateful. And seeing Steponas' pride, awe and joy at the little creature lying in the crib next to her bed, she craved to feel the same.

"Everything will be alright now," he said.

Justine nodded, holding back tears and hoping that it might be so.

Doris took to little Veronika instantly. She cooed and giggled. She gave her finger to the little girl's fierce grip. She glowed at the child in a way that Justine could not. And jealousy tore Justine's heart.

"It's my child," she said, snatching Veronika back. An ugly thought flashed through her mind. *She will love only me.*

"Of course, she is," Doris said. "It's none of my business dear but the more people who love her, the better. Everyone needs love and protection. The small. The weak. People damaged through no fault of their own."

"So now you know everything about children?"

"You are her mother, dear," Doris said, stepping back with a sigh. "Of course you know best."

But I don't, Justine thought with dismay. I don't know best. And I don't want to be her mother.

She stared out at the bare winter garden. The weak sunshine held a false warmth unable to melt ice or bring forth green shoots from the dark earth. It was a mistake to have this child, she thought. A terrible mistake. And cradling the child's head, she put her lips to the thin wispy hair.

∞

Justine started teaching piano, giving lessons on the second floor of Lithuania House. Sitting in the hollow dusty room with creaking floors, bending her head to the children of exiles, she would listen to banging which could do no further damage to the old piano. Listen, she would say, holding a finger aloft. And pacing round, beating time with the ruler, sometimes she would wrap their knuckles.

She played the organ at mass on Sundays and for weddings and funerals. Agreeing without protest, she sat in the choir loft, the soloist beside her. The music grew dull. Pleasure left her. Playing only out of duty, delight disappeared.

She tried teaching her daughter, seating the child on her lap at the keyboard. Pressing first one key then another, she would watch for a reaction. The child twisted and squirmed, wanting to be set down. You're no Mozart, she thought. You certainly haven't inherited anything from me. And standing the child back on the floor, she gritted her teeth against the wailing.

Then one day the student arrived. He was a bright-faced boy with blue eyes, light brown hair and a sky-blue plaid shirt. He was eight. His name was Eddie. And he wanted music.

"So. You like the piano."

"Yes," he said, boldly stepping forward to show what he could do.

Her heart stirred. He had talent. She bent over him. She cupped her hand over his, curling his fingers.

"Like this," she said. "Do you see?"

A smile appeared at the corner of his mouth as the sound grew richer, a private smile meant only for himself. He had forgotten the dusty room, the creaking wood floors, the din of traffic outside. He had forgotten even her, sitting beside him. Captivated, entranced, he was aware of nothing but the music.

"What music do you like?" she asked.

"Mozart," he announced. "I listen to the opera with my father."

Mozart. The god of beauty and perfection, clarity and light. Too easy for children, too difficult for adults. As she knew very well herself.

"You will have to work hard. Very hard. Are you willing to do that?"

"Of course," the boy said turning upon her a look of total surprise.

She hid a smile. "Do you have a piano?"

"Father just bought me one. One hundred dollars. And

mother doesn't like it." He clapped his hand over his mouth with a wide-eyed irrepressible giggle.

Justine had seen the father, a construction worker whose capable hands treated the boy with tenderness. She had seen the mother, a sour woman with a rough touch. She could see the arguments over pennies put aside, saved in the glass jar of the child's future.

"You must practise every day. After school. Will you do that?"

"What about baseball practise?"

"What about music?"

The boy placed a finger to his chin, appearing to give it serious consideration.

"Okay." Then with a mischievous smile he added, "After baseball practise. But please don't forget Mozart."

He placed an arm across his stomach. He bowed. Then he raced out of the room.

Justine looked after him, her mouth twitching with delight. Opening her purse, she took out a crumpled letter, one line on a sheet of yellow paper. *If you are ever in Paris, come and see me.* She heard the faint sound of traffic. She crumpled it in her hand. And tipping her head as if listening to a distant music, she heard the beating of her own heart.

❦

It was like meeting a lover. Leaving peeled potatoes standing in a pot of cold water on the stove, she went out every Thursday at 4 pm. It's not right, she thought, shifting her daughter on her hip, but she couldn't stop her feelings. She wanted to be with Eddie more than with her own child.

The boy's hands fell naturally into chords. His arms lifted in light graceful arcs. He sight-read with no effort. He practised diligently. A gazelle at the piano, he needed only her presence and the odd guiding word.

She would settle down next to him, placing her daughter on the ground. Turning towards the whimpering child, she would shush her. She tried to make her attention rest there. It slid away. Before she knew it, she was back with Eddie and music, Veronika forgotten.

On the way home she would jiggle her up and down on her hip. Unstrapping the thin clinging arms from around her neck, she would set the girl down in the street. Uncle Povilas can toss children up and down in the air, she thought, but I have no such talent. Mine is for making music. And grabbing the child by the hand, she would drag her home.

She would find a husband displeased at having to wait for his dinner. Standing at the stove, boiling the potatoes, she would catch his hostile sideways look. Who's more important? Me and your daughter? Or that boy? And silence settled between them, a no man's land that she made no attempt to cross.

After dinner the child would crawl towards Steponas' feet, trying to clamber up his pant leg. Laying down his newspaper, he would bend down to scoop her up. I can't make myself love you, she thought, watching the child gurgle in his arms with delight. Not in the right way. And knowing that it wasn't fair or right, she would think of Eddie, a bright-faced boy who, one day, would leave her but, until then, was hers.

FATHER GERAS

TORONTO

1953

They had run through the woods, evading soldiers.
Falling to the forest floor, he had pulled his sister down
with him. He had lain atop her, one hand covering her
mouth. Leaves rustled with the footsteps of passing
soldiers. When all was silent again, they had risen,
pulled the twigs out of their hair and continued on.

Run, their mother had said. Take freedom.
Take it, as you take my heart.

She would not come with them. He would not
let himself think of what might have befallen her.
He thought only of his sister and survival.

Later, he heard that she had died not long after
their leaving, and his heart had died, too.

One day, he would return. On bended knee, he would
place flowers on her grave. He would bow his head
and whisper the words that needed to be said.
He would return his heart.

Chapter 1

Father Geras stood on the church steps after Sunday mass, looking out over the hubbub of parishioners. Milling about on the sidewalk, spilling into the street, they had collected in numbers no one had expected. Hopes sharply risen at the news of Stalin's death were beginning to fade. There would be no imminent return home. And letting his eyes linger upon his people, he sensed their restless unease.

Where will I bury them all? he thought. They had survived the war but continued to die.

The church entrance was on Gore Vale Avenue, the rectory on Dundas Street. Rounding the corner, going from rectory to church, he felt as if he were leaving the earthly world for an atmosphere more rarefied. In the peaceful church quiet he moved amid his own thoughts. In this simple space, dreams were kept alive. And returning to the plain two-story brick building, he re-entered daily practical life.

His sister Birute flew out of the kitchen. She flung her arms around his neck, nuzzling him.

"Stop that," Jurgis said, disengaging her with a laugh. A priest could not have his sister nuzzling him, not even at home.

"No, I won't," she said, hanging on in happy mischief.

"That's enough. I have work to do."

"Oh, you're always working. What about me?"

"You have work to do, too."

"Oh, who wants to spend all day cooking for priests? I want to be out in the world like you."

"Don't talk like that. This is a holy place. A house of God. I live here. And so do you."

"Yes, but you go out. I'm stuck in God's house all day long."

Birute, his wayward sister whom he'd caught behind the barn with a farmer's son. Pulling the boy off, sending him packing with a cuff, he'd scolded her. She'd stood swinging her hips from side to side. She'd sucked her thumb. Naughty mischievous Birute, always on the brink of trouble, needing constant watching.

"I'm hungry," he said. "Lunch."

Afterwards he stood in his bedroom, examining himself in the small round mirror above the bureau. Tugging at the bottom of his square-cut jacket, he adjusted the set of his suit. He picked a piece of lint off the dark fabric. He smoothed his black hair. And looking his priestly best, he set off to meet Mr. Lambert, a Canadian with land to sell.

He stepped into the quiet Sunday afternoon street. Tipping his head back, he squinted at the clear sky. The clean Nordic blue was not unlike that of home. The same sky stretches over all of us, he thought, no matter where we are. And putting on his black fedora, he went out in search of a place of rest for his people.

Jurgis never blamed his mother for taking a lover. Living with a harsh husband and four sons moulded in his image, she had turned to her husband's brother for love. Raimundas was kind to her. Jurgis basked in his mother's happiness. And drawing close to her, resting against her once-again pregnant body, he understood that Uncle Raimundas was his father.

His father and uncle fought in the centre of the village, pummelling one another in the dust. Standing beside his mother, slipping his hand into hers, Jurgis had gazed up at her swelling belly. The fight changed nothing except that, after Birute, there would be no more children. Keeping a tight inner circle, they remained a private family of three.

He had entered the priesthood at Uncle Raimundas' urging. Leaving the farm, escaping a father who hated him, and four older brothers who chased and beat him, he was not sorry. He studied but felt no vocation. Giving mild sermons about minor misdeeds, he dispensed good will as best he could.

Birute languished untended. Batted between brothers, forgotten by fathers, she grew ever more wild. Jurgis would return home from the seminary to find his mother frantic and helpless.

When war came his mother would not leave her husband, her first four sons, her first life or her only love. Surrendering to punishment and guilt, she kissed Birute and him goodbye. Think of me, she said. Children of my heart. And turning back towards a life which would become hell without them, she sent them away.

Gerald Lambert was fourth generation, the only son of a wealthy family which had owned a string of mills on the Humber River. Managing the family assets, he supported his two unmarried and uncomplaining sisters, Violet and Maud. For amusement he ran a tavern. When necessary he sold off a parcel of land from the holdings bequeathed by his forebears. It was just such a parcel that Father Geras hoped to buy, a small section now, the rest as the community raised the money.

Father Geras met Mr. Lambert in his tavern, a large ramshackle building on Scarlett Road. Pushing open a plywood door behind the bar, he entered a room smelling of stale cigarette smoke. The dusty desk was stained with beer rings, the red leather of the swivel chair cracked. Despite his family wealth Mr. Lambert appeared not to be profligate. On such details Father Geras' hopes rested.

Gerald Lambert rose from behind his desk, extending his hand. A burly man with red blond hair, freckles along his forearms and small tufts of hair on his knuckles, he seemed decent enough. He was also no fool. Father Geras could see the thoughts rolling through the man's head. A priest was a priest but money was money.

Father Geras asked after Violet and Maud whose names he'd been careful to remember. Assuming an expression of polite interest, he inquired after their health. He was told they were well. Very well. He waited for an invitation to sit down. None came.

"What can I do for you, Father?" Gerald Lambert said, rocking back in his creaking chair.

Father Geras offered a five hundred dollar down payment on an apple orchard lying west of Toronto. Beyond city limits, it would be hard for parishioners to reach. Most relied on the streetcar. Few had cars. But having failed twice to secure land in town, learning afterwards that it had been sold for the same price to someone else, he was settling for the outskirts.

"All very well to offer money for the first piece," Mr. Lambert said, "but how will you come up with the rest?"

Parishioners dropped nickels and dimes into the collection plate every Sunday. Murmuring at the occasional fluttering of a dollar bill, they would crane their necks to see who had been so generous. Poor people who still gave money would keep on giving, Father Geras wanted to say. They were buying their place of eternal rest. Sensing that Gerald Lambert was not a man responsive to poetics, he put it in more prosaic terms.

"We will raise it. We have five hundred dollars now. The rest will come."

"I can't sell piecemeal, Father. I can only sell lock, stock and barrel."

Father Geras fell silent. He had not expected this. He had expected discussion, a graceful dancing around possibilities but not outright refusal. He shifted the brim of his hat through his fingers.

"Father, I know you need the land for a good purpose," Gerald Lambert said. "You DPs are decent hard-working people no matter what others say. I'll give you that. It's just too risky to sell bit by bit. Forgive me for saying so but what if you dig a few holes, stick some people in the ground then can't come up with the rest of the money? Where would that leave me? Part owner of a cemetery half-filled with dead people, that's where." He gave a rough laugh, amused by his own humour. "No one would want it. I'd never be able to sell the rest. I hope you understand my position, Father. Nothing personal. You're a man of the cloth but business is business."

Father Geras sighed. Our families were not rich. We did not come with suitcases full of money. We are starting all over again. We have only our hands and a willingness to work. But he said nothing, sensing that though Gerald Lambert might not be as wealthy as his forebears, he had never been poor.

"You've seen the world, Father," Gerald Lambert continued. "You strike me as a man who knows what's what."

Father Geras had seen the world at its worst. He knew its brothels where young girls serviced military men, its prisons where young men were sent to perish. He had looked into stricken, fear-filled faces. He had held the hands of the dying. Praying over them, he had commended their souls to heaven.

"Our people are scattered by wind," he said. Scattered by the winds of history, he wanted to say but Mr. Lambert did not strike him as a man much interested in history either. "We rest in cemeteries among strangers. We wish to rest among our own people. God will reward you in heaven for your deeds on earth."

Gerald Lambert rolled his eyes. "No offence, Father, but it's earthly matters that interest me. Tell you what. I'll hold the land for six months. You raise the funds. Come back. We'll talk. I'm as good a Catholic as the next guy. Deal?" he said, rising and extending his hand.

"Deal," Father Geras said, taking the man's hand.

Back on the street, he tipped his hat back on his head. Six months. At least the man had not said no. He had been given time. He would find a way.

He found Mrs. Pranaitis in the empty mid-afternoon church, praying in the back pew. Eyes fixed on the large wooden crucifix, knobbed fingers moving along rosary beads, she sought solace. This simple peasant woman in a headscarf was his charge. And he was her shepherd. And settling down beside this aged soul who could not sign her name, he clasped his hands and looked up at the plain wooden body of Christ.

Please God. Help me take care of this poor old woman and others like her. Help me to take care of all of them. Give me guidance to find their place of eternal rest.

No answer came. He did not expect one. God was not a coach who gave private instruction. He gave people strength to find their own way.

Back at the rectory, he was met with Birute's angry shrieks of frustration about burnt suppers and kitchens filled with smoke. Eating the cabbage rolls which she had made a second time, he only half-listened. His mind was on the tasks ahead. A Canadian who needed convincing to part with land. A flock which needed shepherding. A culture which needed protecting. A homeland which needed freeing. And bending to his food, he was determined to find a way.

Chapter 2

———⋅∘◦✿◦∘⋅———

Birute was wilful, wicked, and weak. She wanted what she wanted and didn't see why she shouldn't have it. Life was short. It would be gone soon enough. In this new country, with Jurgis so busy, she was lonely, restless and bored.

There had been that stupid farm boy, pestering her behind the barn. Teasing and laughing, batting him away, she'd finally given in. Look at Mother, she'd wanted to say as she bent to her brother's scolding. For his sake she'd said nothing. Trying to look contrite, she could not help a little grin.

"Birute, you will be the death of me."

"Oh, don't get mad. You love me. Don't you? Don't you don't you don't you?"

"What if, one day, I am not here to rescue you?"

For a moment she fell silent. Then sunshine burbled up in her again. She threw her arms around his neck.

"Oh, but you are."

Birute had gone to Vilnius once, searching for her little girl. Wandering the cobblestone streets, hoping for a glimpse, she had become lost. Jurgis knew where to find her just as he knew most things. He'd taken her home. Tucking her into bed, he had fed her warm milk from a spoon.

"Don't worry," he had whispered as their silent mother fumed behind the shut door. "I will speak to her. She'll relent."

Birute lay in bed sulking that her brother who had such a way with women had become a priest. He could have had a life filled with pleasures, a life in which she could have shared. He had let himself to be shepherded. He had grown pious. And eyes darting back and forth in secrecy, she wished he had not become a priest, a brother no longer totally hers.

No one's going to make me do something I don't want, Birute had thought, sliding further under the covers, her nose resting on its satin edge. No one's going to do that to me.

They had always run together, united against Father and Four Mean Brothers. Even with Mother, he had stood up for her. He had been a priest but still also her brother. He had loved her best. But now, in this new country, he loved church and parishioners more.

⌒≈⌒

Jurgis had taken on Dobilas as caretaker for the church, the Idiot as he was called, even by him though his word was *vargšas*, poor soul. Thinking her brother suffused with too much priestly goodness, she found Dobilas not so much a caretaker as a presence that needed constant watching. But Jurgis had promised. And the job had fallen to her. She resented it but didn't mind the company.

She found him in the basement, sweeping the room used for catechism lessons. Low-ceilinged with a high row of windows that let in a thin strip of yellow light, it had been hand-dug by the previous generation of immigrants. Well, what can I do about it? she wanted to say to old-timers grumbling about newcomers pushing them out. She hadn't asked to be landed here. They would have to move over and make room.

"What do you say, stupid?" she said, leaning against the doorjamb.

"I'm not stupid," he said, moving his broom, his voice dull.

"Yes, you are. But I don't mind."

"You don't?"

"No."

"Then I don't mind about you."

She sucked in her breath. He knew about the baby. Everyone knew, even here. Birute nodded, mute. It only hurt if someone else mentioned it.

He started moving chairs left askew by children released from catechism lessons. Shifting them about, uncertain about where to place them, he seemed lost. *Vargšas*, she thought, her brother's word dropping into her mind. He's even worse off than me. And heart softening, she moved forward to help him.

They worked side by side, stacking chairs. Glancing at one another, they smiled in shy friendliness. When he picked up the broom, she picked up the dustpan. She stooped to hold it steady for him. And watching him sweep, she saw gratitude in every stroke.

⁓

After breakfast, she would make her brother's bed, brush his spare cassock and shine his shoes. Having cleaned up after lunch, she would search out Dobilas in the basement. He would look up with a happy smile. He would set his hammer or paintbrush aside, eager and swift. And hearts lifting they would go out, two friends looking for mild adventure.

They would set out along the south side of Dundas, passing the open green pocket of Trinity Bellwoods Park. Approaching Lithuania House, a broad old building where parishioners had Sunday lunch, they would reach Ossington. At the intersection they would stop. They would look at Dundas dwindling into the distance. Then crossing to the north side of the street, they would turn around and go home.

They would pass Lakeview Lunch, a chrome-grilled diner with no view of the lake. Pressing their noses against the plate glass window, they would peer at the patrons perched on chrome and red leather stools at the counter. They imagined sitting in the high, straight-backed mahogany booths. They would order coffee. And just as they were imagining the easy banter with the waitress and the other customers, the gesticulating owner would emerge.

"Get your snotty noses off my window!"

They would race back to Gore Vale, giggling with delight. Turning into the park, they would make for its heart. They would sit away from the street but within sight of it. They would settle into the comfort of one another's company. And passing an apple back and forth between bites, they would share injustices.

A landlady who had smacked him.

A priestly brother who was never there.

"You like him, don't you?" Dobilas said, a naughty look in his eye.

"It's not like that."

"How then?"

She pondered. "Like a puppy. A puppy that you really really love and want all to yourself."

His vigorous open-mouthed nod of understanding brought spittle to his lip.

"Don't drool. Keep your mouth shut," she said, lifting his chin with one finger.

He clamped his mouth shut in a goofy, light-hearted gesture of happiness and relief. Burrowing against her, his hand might creep towards her breast. He's just a baby, she would think, lifting it away with a gentle kiss. A baby in a male, adult body. And they would sit together, loving but not lovers and no longer alone.

She would return to the rectory, giving Dobilas a parting peck on the cheek. Seeing the unease leap into her brother's eyes, she knew he was thinking of the boy behind the barn. Well, Jurgis had given her the job of watching the idiot. And she was doing it. She didn't want another baby, and certainly not with Dobilas.

One day she overheard Maryte and Jurgis whispering in the vestry.

"I'm worried," Maryte said. "What if they get into mischief?"

"I will speak to her. You speak to Dobilas." Surely he's not *that* much of an idiot, his tone said. *Vargšas.* Poor soul.

Birute withdrew without making a sound. She said nothing to Dobilas or to her brother. Her life was her own. She would not have it controlled by others. She would decide for herself what was right.

One morning, having set her own small room in order, she sought out Dobilas in the basement. Bending over a screen set across two chairs, he was applying a patch to a tear in the mesh. He guided the short stiff wires through holes. He bent them under, tight. Jiggling the patch back and forth, deeming it not snug enough, he stepped back to ponder the problem.

"Let's go for a walk," she said.

He shook his head. "Father Geras asked me to do this today. The mosquitoes bite him at night." He giggled. "He scratches during mass."

"Oh Jurgis can wait one more night," she said, irked that he had not set down his tools, eager and ready for play. And she refused to call her brother Father Geras even in front of others.

"But I promised."

"Well, I'm not going to wait."

I have to be the most important thing to *somebody,* she thought, pausing on the rectory steps, even if only to this idiot man-boy. Doesn't anyone want to be with me?

She stepped into the street, entering the weekday working world. Passing men and women intent on their business, she noticed sideways, not-so friendly glances. What did they think of her? DP—that's what. Well, she might be alone but she was not going to be afraid of them.

She walked along Dundas, passing brown houses, square and opaque. Reaching Ossington and Lithuania House, she went as usual no further. She looked at the pharmacy on the corner across the road. McCann's. And plunging into the intersection filled with traffic and noise, she stepped into the street.

The store's threshold was mosaic, a half-moon of small pink and white stones. Pushing the door open, she entered a golden honeycomb. Cubbyholes ran up the walls from floor to ceiling. Packets and small soft boxes filled every pocket. A white-haired man in a white coat, working behind a chest-high counter at the back, took note of her over his rimless glasses.

Watch if you like, Mr. Pharmacist, she thought, passing up and down the aisles, but I've fooled Nazis and Russians. I can fool the likes of you.

She stopped at the Kotex. He lowered his gaze to his work.

She drifted up and down the aisles, peering at stockings and hairnets and bobby pins. Stopping before the Aspirin, she examined the small metal tins with red and grey stripes. She scooped one up. Hah, Mr. High and Mighty Pharmacist, she thought. What do you think of that? And slipping it into her pocket, she sauntered towards the door.

"Come here, young lady," he said without looking up.

She approached, a naughty child drawn by a commanding parent. Removing his glasses, he pinched the bridge of his nose. He fixed his eyes upon her. His look was stern and direct. It also held kindness and understanding.

"I have three daughters. The two older ones are sensible but the youngest, well, she's always wanting things. Sadie, I say, just because you want something doesn't mean you can have it. Things are not important. It's people who matter. And do you know what else I say?"

Birute shook her head, open-mouthed and feeling a bit like Dobilas.

"I tell her to look around. Look at those less fortunate. Some people have nothing. Not even medicine."

He turned to the cubbyholes, lingering with his back towards her. Suspended in the effervescence of his kindness, she wanted to reach out and touch his shoulder. Your daughters are lucky to have such a father, she wanted to say. Especially that Sadie. And grasping the small metal tin in her pocket, she slipped away.

⌒⊷

She found her brother in his office, working on his sermon. Writing at his desk in his dark cassock, pen in hand, he seemed to her the very picture of a priest. He looked up faintly irritated. He was no longer the brother with whom she had roamed through fields at home. And standing before him, she kept her hand casually yet purposefully in her pocket.

"What have you got there?" he said, looking up.

"Nothing. Nothing that would interest you." She closed her hand over the tin even more tightly, holding onto the goodness a little longer.

"Let me see," he said, coming around from behind the desk.

He pulled her hand out of her pocket. She opened her palm, revealing the purloined tin. She did not resist. She wanted him to see it. She wanted to show the full force of her unhappiness.

"What's this? Where did you get this?"

"The pharmacist gave it to me."

"Oh, he just gave it to you, did he? Don't lie to me, Birute."

"I'm not lying." She lied very well and knew it. She could even lie to herself while pretending not to.

"Stealing. Lying. My own sister. And before the eyes of God, too. What am I going to do with you?"

"Oh quit being so holy. You were just my brother once.

Before Mother and Uncle Raimundas got hold of you. Before you got turned into a priest."

For a moment, he was silent.

"But I am a priest now," he said. He might have become one out of circumstance rather than vocation but in exile, God had granted him a purpose. He had found his true calling. His real work had begun.

"If God is so important to you," she sniffed, "then you go be with him."

"God loves all of us, Birute. He includes you in his grace."

"Hah. First, he takes you away from me. Then you take me away from home."

"Birute," he said, "think of those who have suffered. Those left behind. Those who have died. Those still separated." Every week, the columns of *Tėviškės Žiburiai* were filled with husbands and wives looking for one another, for brothers and sisters, aunts, uncles and cousins.

"You always used to have time for me. Not here. Not now. We always used to be together. What am I to do here without you?" Tears gushed now, words spluttering out along with them. "I'm not going to become an old maid looking after priests. I made a mistake once. And maybe no one will want me because of that," her voice quavered, "but I'm not going to spend my life praying and feeling sorry."

She shook, releasing feelings long held inside, thoughts long avoided.

"What do you want?" Jurgis said.

"Someone who *wants* to be with me."

"But I *am* with you."

"No, you're not. You belong to your parish, to everyone except me."

He sighed. "We are still together. And we are safe."

"We should never have left home."

They stood together in silence, side by side but separate for the first time in lives always lived together.

"We may not be together as we once were," Jurgis said, "but we are safe."

"Maybe we are safe," Birute said, "but we are no longer together."

They turned away from one another, bewildered and discomfited.

Chapter 3

Father Geras thought a priest's duties much like a doctor's, one tending the body, the other shepherding the soul. Following in Dr. Prizura's wake at St. Joseph's Hospital, visiting ailing parishioners, he would feel the clutch of their hands and see the urgency in their eyes. He would offer prayer and comfort. He would administer last rites. And grieving for souls who had reached safety only to depart this earth, he would think of his cemetery.

He entered the room of Mrs. Vitkunas, an old woman pinned to the bed by the relentless sunlight, age and illness exposed by the pitiless bright light of day. Her eyes were shut. She breathed fitfully. As he moved forward, her eyes flew open.

"Oh, it's you, Father," she said, her hand fluttering up towards him. "Thank you for coming to see an old woman."

"God is with you," he said. "He loves you and will take care of you. He will prepare a place for you by his side. He takes all of us into His grace. When we go to him, we see not only Him but all those whom we have lost and loved."

He lowered himself onto her bedside, ready to hear her confession. Listening, he heard her whispers through dry lips. Dear God, he thought. Such small sins, light as air. And making the sign of the cross over her, he felt her sigh of release.

They talked quietly then of the place from which they had come. Holding her hand, helping her to remember, they spoke of the mother and father left behind, the land lost. The skin was loose and freckled. He felt the bones beneath. And running his thumb along the ridges, he wished the hand were his mother's.

"Let us pray to Almighty God Our Father. Let us ask for his forgiveness, his mercy and his love."

They lowered their heads, the sunlight almost forgiving now upon their necks. He led her in prayer, his voice containing the strength of this world, hers feeble with imminent departure. Please God, do not take her yet. Do not let her rest among strangers. And bending his head, he prayed for this poor soul flung to a foreign shore and for his country's freedom.

Father Geras wrote to Bishop Bennett in Montreal, applying for funds to build the cemetery. He described the plight of his people, scattered by war and lost in a new land. He asked the Bishop's kind indulgence. He hoped for the Bishop's beneficent understanding. And calling upon the image of a flock in need of shepherding, he put down the earnest feelings in his heart.

The Bishop sent a polite dry response. The Church had many demands on its purse.

Father Geras took to phoning Bishop Bennett once a week. He informed the Bishop with regret that Mrs. Vitkunas was not getting any better. He pointed out that there would only be more like her. He mentioned the Church's role as custodian. Describing souls tossed about by life and with no imminent prospect of returning home, he conveyed their hope of resting among compatriots rather than strangers.

The Bishop's secretary intercepted the calls. Father Geras must be patient.

Father Geras went to Montreal to see the Bishop in person. Waiting in the Bishop's antechamber, he tried to imagine the life of the young secretary priest. A buzzer on the desk rang. The secretary nodded his permission. And entering the Bishop's presence, Father Geras saw a shrunken old man sitting behind an ornate desk and sunk beneath heavy robes.

"The Church wants to help, of course it wants to help," the Bishop said, sighing with careful patience at this country priest who did not appreciate the delicate dilemma of a Bishop caught between parishes and politics. "But Our Holy Mother Church has many priorities, many demands upon its purse. It cannot be responsible for everyone who comes here from Europe. This is purely a local matter. You and your people must raise the money."

"Surely you mean *our* people," Father Geras said. "Your Holiness."

Mouth puckering, the Bishop said he would see what he could do.

The letters and phone calls kept coming. Wearying of this most polite of squeaky wheels, Bishop Bennett set his own wheels in motion. The right words were put in the right ears. Funds were shifted and reassigned. Returning to Montreal to pick up the cheque, Father Geras bent to kiss the Bishop's ring.

"Thank you, Your Excellency. We will never forget you. You will be remembered forever."

"Yes, yes, I suppose so," Bishop Bennett said, waving him away with a languid air.

Father Geras went back to Mr. Lambert. If the church would provide half now, would Mr. Lambert consider selling? Regrettably Mr. Lambert could not. He needed the full purchase price.

"I'm sorry, Father," he said in genuine sympathy, "but I must consider my sisters Violet and Maud. I must take care of my family."

And I must take care of mine, Father Geras thought. You can't imagine what it's like to be in a new country, alone, while your family suffers back home. Well, you are lucky. But we will find a way. And shaking Mr. Lambert's hand, he thanked him for his time.

The community continued raising money. Women baked cakes, selling them slice by slice after mass. Men whittled wooden figurines, selling them to one another. They bought raffle tickets for books and linens they did not need and could not afford. And as nickels, dimes and quarters grew to dollar bills, Father Geras was humbled by the spirit of a people who had lost everything but continued to give.

⌀⋇⌀

Father Geras had never met Joe Druska, a non-church-goer who kept to himself. Having come in the previous wave of the 1920s, he was a *senas imigrantas,* an old immigrant. He was a bachelor living alone. His age and his past were unknown. Landlord of a house on Dundas, he had a reputation for being solitary and cantankerous.

Father Geras waited on the doorstep, unsure of his welcome. The old immigrants resented the newcomers who had crowded them out of a church that could only hold two hundred. He must be very lonely, Father Geras thought. Perhaps more than most. And peering through the window in the door, he saw a shadow shifting behind the bubble glass.

Joe Druska peered back at Father Geras with distaste. A tall man with fierce eyebrows and an equally fierce personality, he had no fondness for the church. They had not allowed him to divorce his wife. What good was a wife to him back home in Lithuania? He would be tied to the woman forever.

"What do you want, Father?" Joe Druska said, opening the door. He neither minced words nor held with social graces.

"You don't come to church. So I've come to see you."

"The hell you have. You've come for money."

"I won't pretend. The church always needs money. Right now it needs money for a cemetery. But that's not the only reason I've come."

Joe Druska grunted. At least this priest gave a straight answer.

"A cup of tea, Father?" he asked. He was not about to give money but a cup of tea he could manage. And he would let him know just how he felt about the church and its dealings.

Father Geras stepped inside, removing his hat. Looking around the hallway, he noticed the highly-polished wood. He followed Joe Druska to the small well-kept kitchen. No negligence here, he thought. The man had pride.

"You keep a good house."

"Tenants with no complaints are tenants who pay rent."

"Then you must be a rich man," Father Geras said with a good-natured smile.

He's brazen enough, Joe Druska thought. I'll hand him that.

"Not as rich as some. Tea? Or something stronger? You priests like a nip now and then. It must be that Communion wine. And I'm in the mood for a little something myself.

"I'll keep you company. Just don't tell the boss upstairs."

Despite himself, Joe Druska had to laugh.

Joe Druska moved around the kitchen with the familiarity of a bachelor existence. Setting a bottle of rye on the table, he filled two shot glasses. His experienced hand knew just when to stop. The liquid shimmered at the rim. Lifting their glasses in a toast, they drank.

"Why don't you ever come to church, Joe? Perhaps you're a Communist?"

"Never! I don't like company." He had toyed with the idea once, back in Lithuania. Magda had disabused him of it, as she had disabused him of most things.

"Ah."

Father Geras waited.

"So how is parish life, Father?" Joe Druska said. Not that he cared but a man had to have some kind of conversation with a drinking companion. And he felt a sliver of respect for a priest who, despite rumours about politics, had come to see him.

"I can't pretend. They're pretty bad. We have no place to bury people. Not even a place to bury you."

"Oh, don't you worry about me," Joe Druska said, filling the glasses again.

"But I *do* worry. I worry about everyone. Even about *you*. If I didn't, who would?"

Joe Druska knocked back another shot, wiping his mouth with the back of his hand.

"What about your friend upstairs?"

"He worries, too. But it's my job to find the money."

Joe Druska felt the uncomfortable prickle of something he couldn't identify.

"I can't help you."

"And why not?" Father Geras said, looking Joe Druska straight in the eye.

"Because the church has done me no favours," Joe Druska said, holding his gaze.

"Tell me about it."

So this is confession now? Joe Druska thought. Well, he *would* tell the story. He'd tell it so that this priest would go away. He'd tell it so that he wouldn't be bothered again. He wanted to be left alone.

"It was a long time ago."

"In that case begin at the beginning."

"In that case let's have another drink," Joe Druska said, filling their glasses once more.

Joe Druska had come to Canada as a young man, leaving behind his wife and two-year-old daughter. Finding a job in a tanning factory, he scraped bits of raw flesh off stiff hides. He prided himself on sticking with a job that other men couldn't abide. The difficult unpleasant work paid well. And denying himself even drink, he had saved and saved.

I will send for you, he had promised Magda.

And we will come, she had promised. Julija and me.

Joe Druska fetched Magda's letter, tossing it down in front of the priest. Julija, a grown woman by now, likely with children of her own, had never written. That would be Magda's doing. He tried not to think about that.

*I am leaving you. I was never in favour of your going
and now I have an offer of another life here. I'm going
to accept. For the sake of the child. It can never be
marriage but it's better than being a woman left behind
by her husband. And who knows what you get up to
over there. Knowing you, not much and nothing good.*

Father Geras sighed at these ordinary, unnecessary cruelties
of life. No wonder the man kept to himself. He was bitter
and broken-hearted.

"Let me help you."

"No one can help. Not you, Father. And certainly not
God."

"You're wrong. You're a believer. Aren't you?"

"Doesn't matter what I believe," he said, tight-lipped.
"Time for you to leave, Father."

Father Geras rose. "Think about what I've said. No man
wants to die alone. Not even you. Not even tough old Joe
Druska."

Joe Druska sat at the table, looking at a photo after
Father Geras had left. Flexing it, he tried to make the faces
jump. Magda, the only woman in the world he had loved.
Julija, his little angel daughter. And reaching for the bottle,
he drank until he could see no more.

❦

Father Geras made his way to the three small booths at the
back of the church, tucked under the iron staircase spiralling to the choir loft. Passing the line of waiting parishioners, he would see their uplifted, hopeful faces. He could

sense their desire for relief. He welcomed the responsibility that the Lord had placed upon him. And opening the door of the middle booth, its carved open top-half lined with a purple curtain that jiggled with movement, he prepared to hear confession.

The first penitents would enter the booths on either side, lowering themselves to their knees. Waiting until they had settled, he would slide open one of the small panels. *Bless me, Father, for I have sinned.* And looking straight ahead, seeing but not seeing the face visible through the fretwork, he would lean in and listen.

He heard the whispered confessions of grandparents and small children, the sins between husbands and wives. He assigned Our Fathers, Hail Marys, sometimes an entire rosary. He made the sign of the cross. He gave absolution. And sliding the panel shut, he would hear them rise less burdened.

He would return to the front of the church to say mass. Raising his hands in benediction, his wide white sleeves slipping back along his forearms, he would read from ancient and sacred texts. He would genuflect in slow reverence. He would lift the host high for all to see. And suspended within the prolonged ringing of altar bells, the parish clung together in the fierce closeness of a people far from home.

One Sunday after mass, Joe Druska appeared. Ill-at-ease even in the empty church, he came forward, carrying a pillowcase by the neck. He held it out. It was full of cash. And Father Geras's heart began thumping with a fearsome joy.

"One condition," Joe Druska said.

Father Geras waited, desperate for it to be a condition he could fulfil.

"A spot ..." Joe Druska stopped, unable to continue.

"A spot in the cemetery," Father Geras said. "You have my word. I will take care of it when the time comes. A place of honour."

With deep satisfaction and no small pride, Father Geras returned to see Gerald Lambert. Scion of the Lambert family, supporter of two sisters and a good Irish Catholic, Mr. Lambert proved to be a man of his word. Money changed hands. The land was bought. And a dying apple orchard, its wizened trees no longer able to bear fruit, became a cemetery.

Chapter 4

B irute continued to lose interest in rectory life. Shifting her attention to Dobilas, she settled with satisfaction upon a young man who was not constantly telling her what to do. In a world of priests and older brothers, this was no small pleasure. Here was the companion she craved. And watching him sweeping or hammering or rearranging chairs, her heart filled with warmth.

He welcomed her attentions with a sunny, open smile. Going out together, they did not hold hands in this most English city where friendly affection was not shown in the street. Men shook hands or lifted their hats. Women proffered white-gloved hands. And remembering Lithuania where women walked arm-in-arm, Birute missed the touch of bare hands and home.

She and Dobilas walked everywhere for the pleasure of one another's company. Eating ice cream cones in Sunnyside Park, watching the summertime lapping lake, they licked the icy sweetness. They grew ever closer. They became, if not lovers, then brother and sister and friends. And pushing one another on the swings in High Park, they laughed with the gleeful happiness of children.

They would loll on a blanket, Dobilas resting beside her on his back. Propped up on one elbow, she looked down at him. His chest rose and fell in quiet contentment. His eyes were shut. And smiling slightly, he hummed *Žirgelis*, a tune about a young man urging his steed towards a farm gate where a maiden awaited courting.

He may be an idiot, she thought, but he's my idiot. I like being with him.

"Do you want to get married?" she said.

"Yes!" Dobilas said, his eyes lighting up. They clouded over. "What about Maryte?"

"What about her?"

"She's my sister. I can't leave her."

"And why not?" Birute said.

He pondered for moment. "It's like your brother."

For an idiot, she thought, he wasn't so stupid. He understood much.

His face emanated an unhappy helplessness. He would never be able to speak to Maryte. She would have to do it herself. She would have to do it for both of them. And she would have to do it now.

⌒⌒

Maryte opened the door, letting her in with a worried look. Following her up the stairs, Birute noticed the woman's tired, heavy tread. She gripped the handrail to pull herself up. Each step seemed an effort. Standing in the corner kitchen with the small table and two chairs, she presented an exhausted, defeated face.

Birute came straight to the point.

"I want to marry your brother."

"How can you think of such a thing? Can't you see what he is? He's not for marrying."

"Meaning that you don't want him to marry me," Birute said. "But who will have him, other than me? Who would look after him if something happened to you?"

"Nothing's going to happen to me," Maryte said, her manner weary. "I've taken care of him since the day he was born. I will do so until the day he dies."

"Don't you want a break? Don't you want your own life?"

"He is my life. Why do you want to make mischief?"

Birute paused.

"It seems to me that it's Dobilas who gets into mischief sometimes."

Maryte gave her a sharp look but said nothing.

"Until he has someone of his own, there will always be a Mrs. Moynahan."

Maryte continued to remain silent.

"And I can give him something you can't. A baby."

"A baby?" Maryte was aghast. "What kind of baby will the two of you have? And how will he look after it. He can't look after himself."

"Well," Birute said, dryly, "I will be there. Dobilas will look after it the same way he looks after everything else. The church. You. Me."

Maryte still said nothing.

"You are his sister. His family. He won't marry unless you agree."

"*No one* can take care of him as I do," Maryte whispered, tears springing to her eyes.

"Of course not," Birute said, feeling pity for this woman

who would be left on her own, until she remembered the meddling that would likely ensue. "But I can help to take care of him. Could we not take care of him together? Surely two women are better than one."

"You will push me into second place," Maryte said.

"And how can I do that? You have been everything to him since the day he was born. You will always be his sister. He will always love you in a way he cannot love me. I don't want to push you out. If you don't believe me, ask Dobilas. He wouldn't let that happen. He loves you too much. He will always be yours. You will still be able to keep an eye on him. And on me. So. What do you say?"

Maryte's mouth started to quiver with misery.

"What does your brother think of this? Father Geras, what does he think?"

Birute took a risk. Without Maryte's approval, Dobilas would not act. There would be no wedding. There would be no child. There would be no life of her own.

"I don't know. I haven't asked him. I came to you first."

Maryte's eyes widened.

"You came to me first? Really?"

Birute nodded. Then she played her last card.

"Maryte, I ask your permission to marry your brother. Please."

Birute waited. After a time, Maryte nodded.

⌒⊛⌒

The church provided Dobilas an occupation but no pay. Knowing that she would have to make a living for them both, Birute pictured herself going out to work every day. She didn't mind the idea. In fact she rather liked it. And imagining coming home to a meal prepared by her husband, she enjoyed the prospect of having a job, being married and, one day, having a baby.

She picked up the stolen aspirin tin, palm-sized with a dimple catch. Placing her thumb on the red half-moon near the hinge, she sprang it open. Twelve small tablets lay inside, flat and powdery white. Twelve pieces of possibility, untouched, pure as hope Snapping the tin shut and putting it in her pocket, she returned to the pharmacy.

The pharmacist worked behind the chest-high counter at the back of the store, just as before, only head and shoulders visible. Walking around the store, her eyes lingering on the merchandise, she could tell that once again he was aware of her. She approached the counter. She placed the aspirin tin before him. Nudging it with small movements of her fingertips, she edged it forward.

"Forgive, please."

"I suppose you want a job," the pharmacist said, not looking up from his work.

She nodded. How did he know?

"And why should I give you one?" he said, his eyes containing a twinkle of teasing.

Why indeed? Why give a job to a DP who spoke little English and had stolen from him. A slight panic rose within her. Her words came out in a rush.

"Because I sorry. Sorry," she said with earnest sincerity, unable to remember the English for *Labai*. Very.

"And I get married," she burst forth.

"Oh," the pharmacist said, suppressing a smile. "Well then. In that case, I'd better give you a job."

Birute wanted to race behind the counter. She wanted to fling her arms around him. English people did not do that kind of thing. They smiled. They nodded. She gave him a polite thank you.

"Can you do arithmetic?"

She nodded, maintaining a straight face.

"Good. Then you can handle the cash register. You won't need much more than Hello, Thank You, Goodbye. If you have trouble with language, just come to me. You'll learn quickly enough. My name is Miller, by the way. Pete Miller. But you must call me *Mr*. Miller. Especially in front of customers. Do you understand?"

She was struck by the unpleasant thought that, to the pharmacist, she appeared much as Dobilas did to the world. Ashamed that it had not occurred to her before, chagrined at the secret satisfaction of her own condescension, she felt the swift kick of guilt. Dobilas must feel like this all the time, she thought. And a fierce new tenderness rising up in her, she resolved never to tease him again.

"Monday morning. 9 a.m.," the pharmacist said.

"Monday morning. 9 a.m.," she said. "Hello. Thank you. Goodbye. Please come again." She grinned, teasing and cheeky. "*Mr. Miller.*"

Happiness burbled up in her. She began giggling, then laughed, letting loose long ripples that travelled through her body, leaving her in a dazed, pleasurable state. Poor man, Birute thought as her laughter subsided. He really must think he's hired an idiot. And with a friendly wave, she left.

She walked back along Dundas on bouncing steps. Nearing the church, she thought of the good news she was about to impart to her brother. She had a job. She was going to get married. Maryte wasn't going to stop it. Nor, she hoped, would he.

꩜

She waited until dinner when her brother would be settled and quiet, content with her food and company. Cutting the soft beef and pork patties with his fork, he carried the moist soft meat to his mouth. She watched him eat. Someone else would keep him company or perhaps no one at all. And heart sinking, imagining her brother alone, she sat down across from him.

"Aren't you eating?" he asked.

She shook her head, thinking of the parting of daily ways that would take place after her marriage. She would no longer hold up his cassock for him to slip into, no longer stand back to watch as he did up the row of small buttons along the front. A woman would be found to wash his clothes, cook his meals and make his bed. But who would take care of him, her brother priest? Perhaps no one.

For a moment she wavered at the prospect of leaving her brother. He had protected her from indifferent fathers, cruel brothers and an angry mother. They had left home, outwitted soldiers in the forest, travelled across an ocean to a new land. They had kept secret company. They had held together. And never expecting that she would be the one to leave, she quietly told him her news.

He lay down his knife and fork.

"You can't marry."

"Why not?" She had not expected this. She had thought he would be happy, perhaps even relieved to be rid of her and free to work. "Do you mean I can't marry at all, or that I can't marry Dobilas?

"Both."

"And *why* can't I marry him?" she said, bristling at the thought that Dobilas might not be considered suitable, that she might not be free to choose whom she might love, that she might not be free to marry if she so wished.

"Because you will be lumbered with an idiot," he said, his face taking on the distinctly unpriestly look which only Birute knew. "You will have to look after him all your life. What about when you are both old? Have you thought about that?"

"Of course, I've thought about that. I already look after you and the house. I help out in the church. I'll manage. Besides, he's not as stupid as he looks. He understands a lot." Sometimes more than you, she wanted to say.

He struggled as if reluctant to speak.

"What if you have children? What if they are born like him? What will you do then?"

"What of it?" Birute tossed out. She had to admit that she hadn't thought of this before but it didn't trouble her much. How many idiots could one family have? If anything Dobilas would make a more understanding parent.

"But I need you here," Jurgis said, his eyes filling with anguish.

"No, you don't," she said. "Not the way you used to. You have the church. You have your parish. You have your work. I have nothing. I want my own life."

"But I need you to help me."

"Dobilas needs me more."

He fell silent.

"Besides," she added, "I really like him and his idiot ways. He makes me laugh. I like being around him. I can be myself." And he does not judge me, she thought.

His shoulders slumped. Seeing his downcast face, her heart fell, too. Her brother had sat on the edge of her bed, feeding her warm milk while their mother fumed on the other side of the door. He had pulled her to the forest floor, his body covering hers, his hand over her mouth until the soldiers passed. And eyes filling with tears, she moved to embrace him.

"I want to take care of him. The way you have always taken care of me."

"In that case," her brother said, wiping away tears of his own, "you must marry. But only if I get to perform the ceremony."

She hugged him. She would have married Dobilas even without his permission but had the good sense not to say so.

They stood at the sink side by side, doing the dishes. Passing wet plates to Jurgis, she felt the good-natured companionship of a brother who, tea towel in hand, dug her in the ribs at the prospect of becoming a married woman. She would no longer see his smiling face first thing in the morning. She would no longer kiss his cheek last thing at night. And embracing her brother with all her might, she willed into him all the love that she possessed.

Chapter 5

O n a cold grey day in November, Father Geras stood
by an open grave, saying prayers for the dead. Wind whipping at his robes, missal lying open across his palms, he
prayed for the soul of Mrs. Vitkunas. She had breathed her
last, eyes shut, mouth open. Then her beating heart was
stilled. And early snow swirling about him, he laid to rest
the cemetery's first resident.

Communism had settled upon his country like a heavy
cold, a chest cold that nothing could shift and no medicine
could despatch. Surging hopes at the news of Stalin's death
had soon faded. A mood of gritty, open-ended resignation
had set in. And foreseeing the long homeless future, Father
Geras began to plan a more permanent place for his people.

The new cemetery was flat open land, empty but for this
first grave, its modest mounds of earth piled on either side.
Mourners made a silent rim of grief. They clustered together in the cold. And watched over by three old cedars standing like sentinels by a distant fence, they looked down into
the dark chasm into which Mrs. Vitkunas would be lowered.

Leading them in prayer, Father Geras thought of his

mother. Friends recently arrived had brought word that she was dead. Will I ever see where she is buried? he thought. Will I ever be able to go down on bended knee and pay my respects? And imagining her buried under a birch tree, grieving her as well as Mrs. Vitkunas, he felt her beating inside his heart.

Father Geras closed his prayer book, resting it against his chest. Squinting off into the distant emptiness, he saw a shimmering vision. A school, a newspaper, a museum. A new church, halls for commemoration and dancing. And seeing a complex of buildings hovering above this new earth, he beheld his life's work.

They would build on this small patch of land which was now theirs. Working and waiting, keeping hearts and memory alive, they would not forget who they were or where they had come from. They would hope. They would keep faith. And one day, they would go home.

He bowed his head before Mrs. Vitkunas, an old woman who had worked hard, asked little and believed. Returning her bones to the country she had loved, future generations would stand on soil sacred to parents and grandparents, aunts and uncles, brothers and sister and cousins. They would honour those who had left. They would honour those who had stayed. And remembering those who had lived and died, they would honour homeland.

◦✦◦

On an April day mild enough for light dresses out of doors, Dobilas and Birute married. Father Geras had invited everyone, saying that after all he had only one sister and how many times would she be getting married. Dr. Prizura was giving away the bride. Steponas was acting as best man. Justine was playing the organ. And Maryte had agreed to be maid of honour.

Guests hurried up the church steps in the spring morning. Passing the bride, they cast smiles of pleasure at the young woman holding one hand to her veil in the light wind while the maid of honour bent to adjust the bridal skirts. Their hearts were uplifted by the festive occasion. They warmed to the two lost souls who had found one another. And rejoicing in the continuation of life and the persistence of happiness, they went inside to take their seats.

Dr. Prizura, standing in the dim coolness just inside the church door and awaiting the bride, looked at his wife Danguole who sat in a pew upfront, his wife whom he did not love. He had hoped to make her happy but could not. Nor did she make him so. They lived in a no-man's-land of marriage without love. And looking at her sour shifting back, he tried not to think of what did not exist between them.

He thought instead about work, the waiting room filled with patients, the house calls to the elderly, the growing respect at the hospital. He had landed on his feet. He made a substantial contribution to Father Geras' fund for the new community centre. And accepting Father Geras' invitation, he sat on the board of the planning committee.

Danguole complained that she saw even less of him. Unable to give her the attention that she wanted, he hoped the children would keep her busy. Work filled his days. Memories walked through his nights. And carrying the emptiness inside him, keeping it close, he had the company of a pain which became a solace.

He turned at the intimate rustling of women's skirts, facing the door through which Birute was entering. Looking into the bright daylight, he saw a vision in white. He thought of Lidia, his lost love. He saw her eyes. He heard her voice. And offering his arm to the approaching bride, he knew that, while real life surrounded him, the past would always live inside his heart.

Birute, pausing on Dr. Prizura's arm, looked towards Father Geras waiting at the altar, her brother whom she adored. Priestly though he appeared, missal in hand, sturdy brown shoes and trouser cuffs visible beneath the hem of his white and gold chasuble, he seemed once more just the brother who had scolded her and fed her warm milk from a spoon. You will always be mine, she thought. And tears coming to her eyes, she prepared to walk up the aisle.

She had to admit that she wouldn't have minded the presence of her mother. A girl needed her mother by her side on her wedding day but she had Maryte, already the finest mother in the world. I'll be alright now, she wanted to say to her brother, you don't have to worry about me anymore. And thinking of the freedom she was about to bestow upon him, she felt a sunburst of happiness.

She stood serenely holding a bouquet of calla lilies to her waist. Seeing the lit faces of the guests turning towards her, she smiled in private pleasure. I have a surprise inside of me, she thought. And feeling the mischievous delight at a secret about to be sprung, she heard the wedding march start.

Father Geras, watching his sister move towards him and the altar, recognized that look on her face, Birute, his sister who had been a handful from the moment she was born.

Dancing about barefoot on the farm, baiting father and four brothers, she would prance away full of glee. He had been protector and rescuer. Now she would be another man's concern. And catching the wicked flash of eyes within the clouds of wedding white, remembering the finger in her mouth and the sly smile, he admitted how much he liked her company.

He had been busy hurrying out the door, rushing to a meeting or to help a parishioner. Engrossed in his new duties, satisfied with his work, her unhappiness had registered only as a distant sound. She had turned away from him. She had latched onto Dobilas. And seeing his flighty sister poised on Dr. Prizura's arm and on the brink of marriage, he hoped that she would not tire of it and that for all their sakes, it would last.

She had taken the news of their mother's death with a toss of the head. Brushing away the few tears that had leapt, almost a surprise, to her eyes, she had stated that, as far as she was concerned, she didn't care if she ever saw any of them again. You're what matters to me, she had said. And understanding how much he would miss her, he signalled Steponas and Dobilas to take their places.

Steponas, turning to look at the bride, glanced up at Justine seated in the organ loft, his wife whom he had loved upon sight. She did not love him, this woman who sat beside him placid and absent, her touch one of habit rather than affection. She was a broken creature. With time she would mend. And with time surely love would come.

He had hoped that she would adapt, as they had all had to adapt, that a house and children would fill her days. Hoping that she might play, he had bought her an old upright

Heintzman. When would I have time to play? she had snorted. She had seemed on the brink of saying more but bit back
the words. And watching his gift stand untouched, he
sensed her withdrawing even further.

He suggested that Eddie come to the house for lessons,
fearing that it would only take her further from him. She
had flushed with pleasure. She had bent towards the boy in
care and love. And glancing up at her in the organ loft,
Steponas hoped that one day, such love would be bestowed
upon him.

Justine, feeling Steponas' eyes upon her, looked away
from him, her husband whom she could not say that she loved.
He seemed to her a stranger, this man whom she did not
understand and who could not understand her. Yet they had
married. Two children had followed in quick succession.
And waiting for fulfilment, she knew it would never come.

She had watched him presenting the piano, his face
flushed with hope and excitement. Knowing it to be an attempt to buy her love, she also knew then that she would
never be able to give it. You've wasted your money, she had
said. And seeing his face fall, she felt herself ungracious but
unable to be otherwise.

She would stand at the kitchen counter, peeling potatoes
for supper. Digging her peeler into the white starchy flesh,
she would release a wet crumbly spray onto her fingers. She
would see Vilnius and the sunlit studio with the golden
floors, the pearly white baby grand of the Morgensterns, the
audition and Tony Ursell's freckled hand on the nape of her
neck. She would remember Madame Boulanger's letter. *If
you are ever in Paris, come and see me.* And bracing herself
against the counter, she would wait for the moment to pass.

Justine, looking down from the organ loft at Maryte waiting behind the bride, envied the peaceful life to which she would return after the wedding. It was a mistake to give up being single, to marry and have children. She had lost freedom and solitude. She was trapped in the dissatisfaction of second-best. And placing her hands upon the cool organ keys, she released the low groaning moans of the wedding march.

Maryte, feeling Birute move forward at the burst of music, followed her towards the altar where Dobilas stood waiting, her brother for whom she lived. Her weakened mother had passed him to her on the morning of his birth. Take care of him, she had whispered with exhausted breath, he is yours now. And looking down at the new life squirming in her arms, she had felt fierce instant love.

She had sat sewing on the front steps, watching him play in the meadow in front of the house. Eating supper together on their laps as twilight gathered around them, they had pointed up at the benevolent stars. Their mother was one, their father another. They shone down on them. And thinking of her life without them, remembering her liaison with the commandant, she thought of it not just as the price of freedom but as a sort of love.

She followed Birute up the aisle, a woman she did not much like but would learn to live with for Dobilas' sake. Learning to live without her brother would be harder. Please don't forsake me, she beseeched with her eyes as she arrived at the altar. And accepting Birute's bouquet of calla lilies, she stepped aside.

Dobilas, waiting at the altar for his arriving bride, looked past her at Maryte, his sister whom he loved with his whole heart. Catching her anguished look, his heart filled with tenderness for this sister who had been his whole life. Don't worry, he promised with his eyes, I will not forget you. And watching her take her place in the first pew, he hoped that she knew that he would never stop loving her.

Dobilas, taking Birute's hand, faced the altar and his future life. Closing his eyes, he heard the words of ceremony swirling about him. He thought of the old widow and widower leaning together on the fence, pointing and laughing as he spun in the meadow. He remembered Mrs. Moynahan's stinging slap. He remembered Birute finding him and calling him stupid. And standing beside his bride, he felt the luckiest man alive.

They emerged into a morning filled with brilliant sunshine and congratulations. Standing on the church steps, they breathed the fresh spring air. Birute whispered that she was pregnant. His heart began pounding with happiness. And pulling her close, he tucked her hand under his arm.

The assembled guests waiting in Dr. Prizura's garden applauded the arrival of the newlyweds. Taking his bride by the hand, the groom led her out onto the green sward. They began to waltz. They held one another in happiness. And whirling and twirling, tipping their heads back under an eternal sky, they released a joyful shout.

Hah!

Acknowledgements

Thanks to Petra Dreiser, Carole Giangrande and Antanas Sileika for their careful readings of the manuscript.

Thanks to Dr. Jane Howell for her medical expertise.

Thanks to Violeta Kelertas for her unflagging friendship.

Thanks to my editor, Michael Mirolla, for his eagle eye and his guidance.

Most of all, thanks to my parents and grandparents for teaching me about history. May they rest in peace.

About the Author

Irene Guilford is the author of a novel, *The Embrace* (Guernica 1999), and the editor of *Alistair MacLeod: Essays on His Works* (Guernica 2001). Her writing has been anthologized, translated into Lithuanian, and shortlisted for the CBC Literary Competition and the Event Creative Non-Fiction Contest. She lives in Toronto with her husband, Nigel.

Printed in March 2017
by Gauvin Press,
Gatineau, Québec